REACHING
FOR
THE LIGHT

A Novel

by Jan Mitchell Rogers

Grosvenor House
Publishing Limited

This book is published by
Grosvenor House Publishing Ltd
Link House
140 The Broadway, Tolworth, Surrey, KT6 7HT.
www.grosvenorhousepublishing.co.uk

This book is a work of fiction. Any resemblance to
people or events, past or present, is purely coincidental.

A CIP record for this book
is available from the British Library

ISBN 978-1-83975-323-7

DEDICATION

To my husband Clive and all the members
of our extended family

Contents And Timeline

ACKNOWLEDGMENTS

I am extremely grateful to my husband Clive, without whose encouragement and support I would never have been brave enough to put my writing "out there" for the world to see.

I am also indebted to Anne and all the members of the Llanfyllin Creative Writing Group for their ideas and input, without which this book would never have been finished.

Grateful thanks are also due to my friend Hilda for kindly assisting with editing.

Prologue – February 1899

I remember it was very cold and my new leather boots were hurting my feet. The mistress had made me a present of these as her daughter, Miss Susan, did not like the design, but I would have been better on the frozen, rutted track in my old ones, even if the soles were thin and worn. I had a half day holiday from The Plas, where I worked, and could usually manage the three mile walk back to the farm my father rented from the Estate in about an hour. Today, however, the weather was against me. Lying snow had compacted treacherously on parts of the track and it was starting to snow again, flurries coming so quickly now that I began to wonder if I would manage to get home at all.

I was so pleased to find work at The Plas. Sir Reginald had told my father about the opportunity when I was 15 and we were so happy. Our farm was quite remote from other places of work, and to be able to gain a place within walking distance of home was too good to be true.

I had been working there for three years now as a parlour maid, but I had some news to give my mother and father too. Miss Susan's personal maid was leaving The Plas to marry a footman who worked at their house in London and would be moving down there. The mistress had said I could have her job when she left, which would be a great opportunity for me. Miss Susan and I were a similar age, and she seemed to enjoy chatting with me. I was excited. We were lucky to have such thoughtful landlords here. The tenants in other local estates were not nearly so well looked after as Sir Reginald's.

I was looking forward to the new work. It would be much easier than clearing the fireplaces each morning and the other parlour chores. I would have a better position too, as well as a bigger salary. As a lady's maid I would almost be a lady myself, and I could give more money to my parents to help with the costs of bringing up my brothers and sisters.

The snow was coming faster and thicker now. My parents would be worrying about me in this weather. Suddenly, I heard the slow footfall of horses walking on rough ground, and the creaking of a cart. I peered behind me through the curtain of falling snow until I could make out who was coming down the track. Finally, as it drew almost level with me, I could see that it was William Owens, the Miller, taking deliveries to his customers.

As it reached me, the driver leaned down to talk to me.

"Well, its 'Lady' Sarah," he leered at me. He had insulted me in the past, calling me too big for my boots, and worse. He said I thought I was too good to pass the time of day with him.

"Where are you off to today?" he asked, though he must have known I was on my way home. The track here only led to my father's farm.

I did not like the miller. I remembered once at the local fair when he had been drunk. He had grabbed at me, and tried to kiss me, his foul breath making me feel sick. I had pushed him away, but I felt he had always had a grudge against me after that encounter.

I did not trust him, but the weather was getting worse and I began to fear for my life in the blizzard. It was so easy to get lost in driving snow, and perhaps never be seen again. It would not hurt to be polite to him, I thought.

"I'm going to my father's for tea," I told him.

"Well, why don't you jump up on the cart. I'm heading that way myself and you will get there much quicker."

I did not like the expression on his face, although his words sounded polite enough. With the weather turning so bad, I might not make it home at all.

I decided to accept his offer as gracefully as I could, but I knew I had to be careful. As he handed me up into the cart I tried to keep as much distance from him as possible, but I never dreamt what would happen next.

PART ONE - 2019

CHAPTER ONE

It was a good time for new beginnings, Amy told herself, as she pulled up the blinds and opened the office window to let the breeze blow in. The sunlight sparkled on the amethyst ring she wore on her left hand in memory of Matthew.

The winter had been changeable, some very cold weather in January, followed by unseasonably warm weather in February. March had brought heavy rain and dark skies, and Spring had seemed a long way away.

Amy was tired of the winter lethargy. The bright April day offered rejuvenation and hope. The March floods had abated, the river level returning to normal, and Shrewsbury was beginning to get back to its best now in the Spring sunshine.

Luckily, the flood water had not reached her own property, the lease for which she had taken out in January. She rented a small two-story terraced former cottage, situated on a rise a short way from the riverbank and between the town and The Quarry. The quiet street was lined with trees and there was a footpath down to the riverbank and through to The Quarry itself. She loved the location as it seemed to offer the best of both worlds, quick access to the town on one side, and the benefits of the natural world - birds, trees, and trim parkland - to the other.

She stepped out on to the pavement to review her handiwork. She had finished the exterior painting two days before but just needed to polish up the door furniture.

"You've made a good job of the decorating." Rob, her neighbour from two doors down, was turning the key in his front door, and glanced around to admire both her handiwork and the young woman in front of him. With her red-gold curls and green eyes she could have walked out of a pre-Raphaelite painting, he thought. He was beginning to get to know her quite well now. He had assisted her with carpentry on some of the internal changes she had needed to make. She intrigued him, but he felt she was keeping him at a distance, not letting him in.

She had altered the layout of the cottage so that there was an office downstairs and a small one-bed flat on the first floor. She had had to restrict the changes she would have liked to make, as the property was only rented, but she had been given the landlord's permission to move the kitchen up to the upper floor.

She had just left a small cubbyhole to hold a sink and worktop for a kettle etc. at ground level. One of the two upstairs bedrooms had been made into a small lounge, with a gallery kitchen in a recess on one side, and the other retained as a bedroom which was just big enough for her small double bed.

Rob had fitted shelves into the office area downstairs and had built in some cupboards in the lounge and bedroom to help with storage, which was something of a problem. Luckily the cottage, although fronting directly on to the road, had a small courtyard back garden which contained a sturdy shed, ideal for keeping those of her belongings which would not fit either into the office or the flat.

Rob was in his late 20's and was an actor by profession, with a few TV appearances to his credit and some small theatre roles, but in between 'proper' jobs as he thought of them, he would take on carpentry and other handyman jobs to supplement his erratic income. He had enjoyed getting to know Amy as he worked on renovating the building.

She had grabbed his attention from the day that she took over the lease on the property and he hoped he might have a chance to get to know her even better. She did seem withdrawn though, as if wrapped up in her own little world, and he did not want to ruin the chance of a relationship with her by rushing things and frightening her away.

As for Amy, she assumed that anyone with his tanned good-looks, brilliant blue eyes, and well-toned body, must be already spoken for. For this reason, she had not even considered he might be romantically interested in her, and she was still far too involved with Matthew to consider him as a potential lover.

She was grateful for the compliment about the decorating and shook the hand he held out to her. She was proud of her achievement and it felt good to have someone else appreciate her efforts. This had been her dream, to set up her own business and make full use of her gift. To be fulfilling that dream before she reached thirty was wonderful.

She had resigned from her job at the Museum at the end of December. The New Year felt like the right time to start her new venture. She felt excited but anxious.

In the past, her gift had been her hobby not her livelihood, and now she could not help being apprehensive. She did not doubt her ability to communicate with 'the other side', but just how useful paying clients might find that communication was debatable. She might not be able to make a difference for people, and if she were being paid on results that could be a problem.

She had no doubts whatever about her gift. From a young age she had seen figures that had been invisible to other people. It had been confusing at first, and she had learned not to talk too much about these encounters as they made those around her uneasy.

When she was seven years old, her parents had been killed outright when their car was shunted between two lorries on the motorway. She had been in the classroom at school at the time and knew instantly what had happened as they both appeared beside her in the room.

"Don't be too upset, Amy. We will both still be here whenever you need us."

When her Auntie Susan arrived two hours later to collect her, mascara streaked down her cheeks and eyes newly wet at the thought of telling Amy what had happened, she and the teacher were amazed at her calmness.

Several days later Aunt Susan had taken her to the local surgery.

"We are really worried about her – she hasn't even cried since she heard the news."

The doctor had talked to her gently but seemed satisfied with her answers.

"I don't think she has been damaged by the shock," he said. "Children can be very resilient. She may just have a very calm nature."

Young Amy, listening to his comments with interest, thought he could not have been more wrong. There was nothing calm about her inner life. She was always being disturbed by other entities, and voices trying to gain her attention. It was only the cast-iron certainty that her parents were still looking out for her that gave her any peace. Gradually she had learned to screen out as many of the voices as possible, like tuning a radio, and only pay heed to those she wanted to hear.

Rob realised her thoughts were miles away and turned back to his own cottage, murmuring a quick farewell. She nodded goodbye distractedly as he went, intent on polishing the brass plate she had asked him to fix to the wall next to the front door.

AMY RAE

Psychic Consultant

She had not known quite how to describe her gift but thought this job title would at least attract the attention of the curious if nothing else.

Her previous experience had been mainly giving tarot readings to friends and acquaintances, and appearances at charity events where she would do readings and split the proceeds 50/50 with the charity concerned. She was always conscious of the need to keep things light on such occasions. No-one wanted to be frightened silly at a charity fundraiser.

For this reason, she used a tarot deck from which she had removed both the Death card and the Devil, as most people found these cards terrifying. It did not make much difference to the readings, she felt, as there were other cards that evoked much the same meaning – change and a new path which the Death card signified, and opposition and temptation, signalled by the Devil card – but she could take a gentler, less frightening approach with her clients.

It was mainly women who came to her for readings, concerned with events in their emotional lives. The Full Moon could be interpreted in much the same way as the Death card, except she could use it as a way to suggest the opening up of new beginnings, and there were other cards that could be read in a similar way to the Devil, but would seem less threatening.

She would also give readings based on astrology and star signs. The women who came for tarot readings tended to be interested in, or curious about, all aspects of the paranormal. Many of them were seeking to resolve dilemmas in their lives and needed a push to move things on from a situation that seemed to be stuck in some way.

Occasionally she would do a reading for someone who made no connection with her whatsoever. Perhaps they were blocked themselves or did not want to share their inner life in any way. When nothing came to her, she would usually start the reading with the stock phrase "You are at a crossroads in your life,". It was amazing how the barriers would then go down and she could 'get through' to her client in a much more open way.

She had placed ads in the local newspapers, giving her office address, landline, and mobile phone numbers, and hoped that word of mouth following her charity appearances would help to get the business off the ground. She was still working on a website which she hoped would eventually lead to more business.

'I just have to get on with it all now,' she thought.

The office looked established and professional. She had been sourcing furniture from local antique shops and managed to find a heavy mahogany partner's desk with green leather top that she felt made a perfect centrepiece for the effect she was trying to create. She had also found a solid oak bookcase on which to keep her box files. She had her multi-purpose laptop which fitted neatly on top of the desk, with a printer stowed on a table in the corner of the room, and the wi-fi box perched on the top of the bookcase with the landline phone, but she still believed, particularly in her line of work, that paper records would be important as points of future reference if required. She also collected cuttings from newspapers on strange or paranormal events as background to her work.

Two ladder back chairs and two armchairs, rescued from someone's skip, and recovered in antique brocade by her own efforts, made up the rest of the furniture, and the curtains framing the window were in the same burgundy and silver fabric as the chairs.

Paying six months' rent in advance, redecorating, and furnishing the office had taken up much of her available budget. The upstairs flat was furnished with items from her previous home, a bedsit above a local newsagent on the outskirts of the town. At least she had the small double bed and some storage for clothes. Decorating and furnishing it as she wanted would have to wait until she had earned some income. Rob had helped her with the trickier tasks, but she had enjoyed doing most of the work herself, as it gave her the opportunity to use her own creativity and self-expression.

Over the years since her parents' death, she had gradually put a little distance between them. The idea had probably come from them, she thought. They implied that she deserved to live as normal a life as possible. If she were still too close to them it would prevent her enjoying other relationships. She had got on well with Aunt Susan, who had brought her up and formally adopted her. It must have been hard for a woman with no previous experience of children to suddenly have a seven-year-old to deal with, she thought.

Aunt Susan had certainly tried to be a good guardian, but she was sadly lacking in imagination and could not cope with any of Amy's 'nonsense' as she called Amy's contacts with the 'other side'. Amy had grown up learning not to talk too much about her gift, and it was only after meeting Matthew that she felt she could really discuss it with another living person.

Once she had distanced herself from her previously ever-present parents, Amy had begun to form other relationships in the 'solid' world, as she called it. Three years previously she had met Matthew, her lecturer at night-school, and he had understood better than anyone else in her life what her gift really meant.

It had been Matthew who had persuaded her to give tarot readings and one-to-one consultations at charity events, which had broadened her profile and encouraged her to interact with other people in a meaningful way.

"You should not waste your gift," he told her, "It could be of real help to people in need if you use it wisely."

This whole venture was due to Matthew, she realised. Although she was only renting the property, it was the legacy he had left her that enabled her to give up her day job at the museum and start to take her gift seriously. His money would at least tide her over for the first few months' expenses, and if all else failed, the museum had said they would be glad to have her back again.

She had met Matthew through a further education class years after leaving school. She had wanted to get her tech skills up to date and had enrolled for an evening class of which Matt was the lecturer. He was twenty years older than her, but they had hit it off straight away. What attracted her to him most of all was his open mind. He was prepared to accept things he might not be able to see, as well as being intelligent and very well-read.

She did fancy him too, she recalled with a smile. His silver-flecked hair hung quite long over his collar in an arty kind of way, and he had the kindest hazel eyes she had ever seen. He had tried to keep their relationship light at first, but she knew he was 'the one'. Something told her that they had known each other before. In a previous life? It was possible, although Matt was sceptical. She just knew that whenever she saw Matthew she started to smile, and if by chance they met away from the college, unexpectedly, it would light up her whole day.

For several weeks they went for a drink after the class had finished. They would talk about books they had read, music that they loved. They both shared a passion for the musical Les Miserables, and Puccini arias, and their taste in fiction ranged from crime to classics, with everything from Neil Gaiman to Hilary Mantel in between.

Amy was anxious to move the relationship forward, but Matthew seemed strangely reluctant. Worried about the age gap, she wondered, although she knew that would not be a problem for her to deal with. Finally, after the last evening class of the term, he suggested they go back to his flat.

"I have something to tell you," he said seriously.

She was hoping this was the chance to take their intimacy further, but his expression worried her.

He poured her a glass of her favourite red burgundy as they sat in the simply furnished living room. Bright and airy with a turquoise Scandinavian-style three piece, a small pine dining table with two chairs and a pretty Monet print on the wall above the log burner, it made her feel at home.

"What was it you wanted to say to me, Matthew?" She took a sip of her drink as she waited for his reply.

"Well, I thought you should know, before we take our friendship any further – I have a long-standing health problem. That is the reason I changed careers and started teaching adult education classes. There is a problem with my heart. I might go on for years, but I might drop dead in five minutes time with no warning. The doctors are unable to say which is the more likely."

Amy took his hand in hers reassuringly. Somehow the news did not come as a huge surprise. She had intuitively picked up something from his manner. Perhaps it was her unconscious sensitivity to his condition that had generated her attraction to him in the first place.

"We mustn't let that bother us," she murmured. "Part of a satellite could fall out of the sky on top of us at any time as we walk down the street. We cannot put our lives on hold just in case something awful happens. Think of all the joy we would miss if we did."

She did not tell him of the many times she had had to suppress flashes of prescience, things that might or might not happen in the future.

Matthew laughed. "I suppose you are right. We should just make the best of the time that we do have."

She pulled him up from his chair, and led him into the bedroom, laughing.

Amy came back to the present with a shock, a sudden shower of rain beating against the fresh green paintwork of her front door. She hurried back into the office, closing the door tightly behind her and shutting the open window. With a smile she remembered his tender lovemaking, so different from her previous, younger lovers. Although athletic, the younger ones had always made her feel as if she had had a work-out in a gym, whereas with Matthew she felt genuinely loved, body and soul.

It had been over a year now since he had passed away but his legacy had made all this possible, and in some ways she felt closer to him now that he had passed over than she did before. She did sometimes long for his physical presence, but at least she could still talk to him and confide in him, even if it were all just in her mind.

She spent the rest of the morning sorting out her office. She filed away the notes of the few cases she had investigated on a semi-amateur basis. At 1 pm the telephone rang, and she jumped in surprise. Her gift had not forewarned her of that, she thought.

The male voice on the end of the phone sounded quite young, which surprised her a little. Most of her previous clients had been women on the wrong side of middle-age, wanting to contact elderly parents or partners who had passed over to the other side.

"Hi, is that, um, Amy Rae? I'm Sam Johnson. I wonder if you can help us."

She listened as he outlined the case. A young girl with 'an invisible friend'.

"Yes, I think I can help," she did not want to sound too eager. "I could come out to you next Wednesday if that will be okay. Although it might take me at least two days to discover what is going on."

"How much do you charge?" he sounded hesitant.

"I'll email you with my terms. You can email back if you agree and I will then put Wednesday in the diary. As I am still building up a reputation, I will not bill you until you think the matter has been resolved, or at least improved."

As she put the phone down, she hugged herself. A case on her first day of working professionally. "Let's hope it all works out," she thought. She did not doubt her gift but sometimes it could let her down. Happenings 'on the other side' were rarely straight forward.

She turned and glanced out of the window. The rain had stopped now, and the freshly washed street was sparkling in the cool sunshine. The pansies in the window box she had placed outside glowed yellow and purple with the hope of Spring and Summer to come, and she hoped that was an omen of success.

CHAPTER TWO

"I'm sorry Maggie. I just could not go on any longer."

Maggie awoke suddenly, drenched in sweat. Her sister's face was still sharply before her, as clear as it had been when last she saw her, twenty-five years before.

Her fever was turning to chill now, her skin clammy and her pulse racing. She grabbed the burgundy velour dressing gown from its hook by the pine-framed double bed and wandered into the kitchen to make a warm drink. She knew her mind was far too active to return to sleep just yet. As she filled the kettle and put it on the stove, the clock above the Rayburn showed 1.45: still hours to go before morning, the night had hardly started yet.

A movement outside the window caught her eye – there on the main road across the valley were two fast moving vehicles flashing blue lights that pulsed through the darkness. She could not tell if they were police cars or ambulances, or one of each, but at this time of night they spelled trouble for someone.

She shivered, remembering previous occasions involving police cars and ambulances – always bad news for someone. She remembered the visit from the police when she was seventeen. Her father was late home that night and she, her mother and sister, had already started to worry, but the news that they had brought was worse than they had anticipated. Their lives had been shattered by his death, and that was the beginning of Ellie's troubles, Maggie decided.

The whistle of the Rayburn kettle as it boiled jolted her back to the present and she made herself a cup of camomile tea, her usual remedy if she needed help to relax. As she walked back to the lounge, cup in hand, she caught sight of herself in the full-length hallway mirror. Despite all the trauma of the last quarter century she was not looking too bad for a woman with a son of nearly 30, although she realised with something of a shock that so much of her life had passed her by in a haze of grief and guilt. So many years wasted in regret and heartbreak.

Despite her internal turmoil, she had always tried to keep up appearances. The clothes she bought were smart and business-like, and she had her hair cut and coloured at a salon in Shrewsbury to keep the grey at bay. She had tried to keep an eye on her figure too, but during her forties weight had crept on, and she could really do with losing a couple of stone, she thought wryly. Those twice weekly coffee and cake sessions with her friend Laura at the farm next door had caused the trouble, especially as she could not resist Laura's home-made Battenburg cake. If it were not for her hard work keeping the gardens at the Mill neat and tidy, and regular workouts at the gym in Welshpool, she would probably be a lot bigger still. Her working life these days consisted of keeping the Nant-y-felin holiday complex running efficiently, as well as helping her son Sam with some of his estate management. She was also involved on voluntary basis with some of the village activities and was currently Treasurer of the local Flower Show.

Sometimes she felt 'Keep calm and carry on' should have been her mantra, but very few people were aware of the effort she made to show this calmness to the world, when underneath her emotions and anxiety were constantly churning away.

She sat perched on the edge of the sofa in the lounge and let her mind wander back to her sister. The dream had reinforced all those memories that had never gone away, and the fear that she had not been there enough for Ellie when she was most needed. She had tried to bury the feelings and get on with her life but in reality she realised now that she would never really be able to move on until she had properly faced up to what happened and her own role in the tragedy all those years before.

Ellie was four years younger than Maggie – the baby of the family. She had always seemed vulnerable, right from the very beginning. Fae, somehow, and dreamy, almost as though only a part of her were here on earth and the rest of her was somewhere else entirely. She had been terribly spoilt, the darling of her father. When he was killed in the tube train accident when she was 13, Ellie had been inconsolable, and it had made her more sensitive than ever. Maggie, as the older sister, had always felt responsible for her somehow. It was probably a continuation from childhood. Her mother had been ill for a brief period when Ellie was tiny, and her grandmother had come to stay and look after them all. She had told Maggie when she was about five years old that she should look after Ellie, and somehow this seemed to have turned into her life's work, and was a feeling she had never been able to shake. She had read in a magazine somewhere that it was a feeling common to many elder siblings – 'the elder child's burden' they had called it. Later when she was in the final year of junior school, her father had had a nervous breakdown and her mother had told her she must be a good girl to help out and look after Ellie, reinforcing the earlier message.

Occasionally she did rebel though, and it was when her cousin Sylvie was around that she had had the chance to break out.

Ellie was most put out when Maggie's time was spent with a cousin of the same age as she was, rather than looking after her younger sister.

It was probably the fact that everyone (except perhaps Sylvie) wanted to protect Ellie when she was growing up that had led to her increased fragility as a teenager.

It was this vulnerability that had first attracted Steve when he returned from working abroad. Ellie was 18 by then, beautiful in an elfin, childlike way. Slim, neat-featured and with white-blonde pixie-cut hair she had appealed to his instincts to protect and nurture.

While her fragility was attractive, at least at first, it also made her insensitive to the pain of others, and self-absorbed in her own problems. She had no idea that she had broken Maggie's heart.

Maggie had loved Steve since they were both five years old and met in infant school. They lived in adjoining streets in North Chingford and would often walk home from school together. When they were a few years older they would roam in a nearby part of the forest, in the long summer holidays, playing Robin Hood and Maid Marian while only a few minutes' walk from home, and within shouting distance of their respective houses. Being four years younger, Ellie was too young to go out to the forest to play with them. She used to cry to be allowed to go as well, but there was no way her mother would allow it, so it was always Steve and Maggie, and even then Maggie had felt he was the one for her. She could not conceive of a future without him in it.

Their friendship cooled when they went to separate secondary schools, but Maggie had always hoped it would be renewed. During her teenage years, she had never looked at another boy when Steve was anywhere near. Steve had been oblivious to Ellie while she was growing up considering her, when he thought of her at all, as something of an irritation, and he had taken Maggie's obvious devotion completely for granted.

Maggie had left school after taking 'A' levels and then trained as a library assistant, working at first in London, commuting to Liverpool Street from the handy mainline station. Chingford was the end of the line and she would get to the station early and wait for an empty train to arrive in the mornings. This made the commute much more bearable as she always had a seat on the train. She loved working in the City, but did not like the tube, her father's fatal accident never far from her mind, so she would do a fifteen minute walk from Liverpool Street to Cheapside where the commercial library which employed her was based. She adored the feel of the ancient buildings, interspersed with the new modern blocks, and could almost feel the history floating in the motes of the dusty air. Her walk would take her through a lovely green square which she called 'the oasis', a calming place before the day's work began.

Steve had returned to Chingford when he was 22, after touring abroad with a budding rock band for a couple of years. Maggie was still living at home and commuting every day. She had thought of renting somewhere closer to her work, but the rents were so high in Inner London and the commute from Chingford was painless. Coming home she would sometimes stay on in the library for a while to avoid the main rush hour panics, and catch a later, emptier train from Liverpool Street.

On Steve's return, Maggie had been expecting to at least renew their friendship as his parents still lived in the next street, but she never dreamt that he would be captivated by her little sister when he saw her fully grown.

His parents had thrown a welcome home party for him to which Maggie and Ellie had both been invited. He was standing in the kitchen pouring himself a drink when the sisters arrived. Maggie was a little ahead and he had seen her first, admiring her 'all grown up' in her well-cut but sensible trouser suit, and neat auburn bob, and was quite happily chatting away to her when Ellie walked in. She was wearing a satin and chiffon concoction which upstaged every other woman in the room, while enhancing her ethereal beauty. Once he had caught sight of her Steve was under her spell completely. She could see it in his eyes and even now, all these years later, the thought still gave her pain.

Maggie had always found it difficult to express her feelings. Perhaps because of the pressure on her as a child she had never been very demonstrative. Even much later, when her son, Sam, was a small child, she had to almost force herself to give him regular hugs so that he did not grow up with the same reluctance to show affection.

Being unable to adequately express her feelings did not mean that they were any less deeply felt, however. She had always found it almost impossible to cry if anyone else was in the room and bottling up her emotion often made her feel like a volcano about to explode.

'Love' was the furthest Maggie could ever go in terms of endearments, even reserving this for those closest to her. Ellie was the complete opposite. She was always hugging and kissing and called everyone 'hun' (her version of honey) from the very first meeting with them. This affectionate response, combined with her attractive vulnerability, made it almost impossible for anyone, male or female to resist her, at least initially.

Maggie found herself remembering the torment of Ellie and Steve's wedding, more than thirty years ago now. She had tried to carry the day off with a beaming smile but inside her heart had been breaking. What made things worse was the fear that Steve and Ellie were not really suited to each other at all. Once the fairy-tale wedding was over, she dreaded how her sister would cope with the reality of marriage.

Ellie had asked Steve's father to give her away. She had known his Mum and Dad for many years as they were almost neighbours. Maggie worried that her mother would be hurt that she did not ask Richard. Some years after their father's death, Angela had become friendly with Richard, although she had tried to keep the relationship low key at first due to Ellie's sensibility. By now Richard had become a major support in Angela's life, although Ellie refused to acknowledge him as any kind of substitute for her dead father.

In the run-up to the wedding, Maggie had tried to bring up the subject with Ellie. She was helping her to try some different make-up techniques, and suggested a softer, pale turquoise eyeshadow to enhance her eyes.

"You know, love," she tried gently, "it would make the wedding a much happier day for us all if you could find it in your heart to be more accepting of Richard. Mum does find him such a comfort, and he is devoted to all of us."

Ellie was dismissive. She obviously did not want to think about it.

"Oh, I'm sure he's kind enough in his way and I suppose he is good for Mum, but I can't understand how she could replace Dad with someone else. It is too much to expect me to treat him like Dad. I miss him so much and he would have loved to see me getting married. It is so sad that he will not be around to see me on my special day, or to give me away." Ellie brushed away a tear but was careful not to smear her mascara.

"Yes, love, but is it fair to expect Mum to carry on alone after all this time? Don't you think she is entitled to some happiness after all the sadness she has been through?"

"All I know is that if I had a husband like Dad, who had died in such a tragic way, I would never want anyone to take his place. And, anyway, it has not been that long. It's only five years after all."

'Nearer six,' Maggie thought but did not want to add fuel to the fire. She realised she was not getting very far but hoped her intervention would at least make Ellie more civil to Richard on the day. As far as the 'giving away' was concerned Ellie was unshakeable, and Steve's father did the honours as originally planned.

Maggie replayed the wedding in her head as if she were watching a video. She found it strange how clearly she remembered every detail, from her vantage point as chief bridesmaid behind the couple. She had been wearing a lacy pink dress which did not suit her personality at all, but which fulfilled Ellie's idea of her dream wedding.

Ellie did look beautiful, she had to admit. Her hair was a shining white-blonde cap threaded through with a delicate diamante tiara, from which hung a short, filmy veil. Her dress was off the shoulder in satin studded with seed pearls, and she carried a small bouquet of pink and white roses.

Steve had looked proud and protective in his dark grey suit as he stood next to her at the altar and they exchanged their vows.

The reception was difficult. Maggie and the other two bridesmaids (Ellie's old school friends), and Maggie's mum were all on the top table with the bride, groom, groom's parents and best man, but Richard had been airbrushed out of the picture, and was seated a side table with their cousin Sylvie and various, more distant relatives.

Maggie had suggested to Ellie that she ask Cousin Sylvie to be a bridesmaid, but Ellie was not keen.

"She wouldn't fit in with the scheme I had in mind."

Maggie felt it was more than that. As Sylvie was another blonde, Ellie was afraid of being upstaged, not that there was much likelihood of that.

Despite her own pain, Maggie could see how awkward it made Richard feel being seated away from her mother, and how difficult it was for Angela, who was bravely trying to carry off the slight so as not to upset Ellie's big day.

Maggie realised that going over these old memories was just causing her more pain. She drained the rest of her cup and wandered back to bed, hoping that sleep would not elude her for too long.

Once she returned to bed, however, the dream was still vivid in her mind, and she re-examined the events that had led up to the terrible day when Ellie died.

Ellie and Steve had married when Ellie was barely nineteen. Maggie, despite her broken heart, decided to be sensible and not allow it to ruin her life. The following year she had married Paul, the Deputy Librarian at the local public library to which she had transferred after the commercial library in the City had closed. He would never be the love of her life, she realised, but he was hard-working and sensible. She could do a lot worse and maybe she would come to love him properly in time, especially if he gave her children. She could never envisage life without children of her own.

A few years after the wedding her mother and Richard had emigrated to Australia. Angela had been sad to leave the girls, but Ellie's rejection of Richard had really upset her, and once the girls were both married, she felt they could fend for themselves.

"I'm sure you will both be fine," her mother had told Maggie, "and maybe if things go well you can come out and visit us from time to time."

Maggie had heard the unspoken reservation. Her mother did not expect Ellie to come.

"Of course, if there are grandchildren, I will probably have to come back ...." Angela had laughed ruefully.

Maggie felt another sharp pang of grief remembering the conversation. Her mother had had a sudden and unexpected heart attack within six months of emigrating and had never had a chance to see her grandchildren.

Two months before the arrangements for the emigration were complete, her mother's solicitors had been in touch to tell Angela that a distant relative had died and left her a semi-derelict Mill, with a range of rundown outbuildings and 10 acres in Montgomeryshire.

"Richard and I are not going to change our plans now, so I have decided to put the property half in your name and half in Ellie's. It will be for you decide whether to keep it or sell it on, although it could be a brilliant opportunity for anyone prepared to put in the work."

Maggie was overwhelmed and gave her mum a big hug.

"Are you really sure that's what you to want to do, mum?"

"Positive, but I really hope it will bring you and your sister happiness."

Maggie and Ellie had discussed it thoroughly with Paul and Steve. They all decided it was the opportunity of a lifetime and they must at least go and look to decide whether renovating the Mill would be a viable project that they could all commit to.

Tossing and turning, with all these memories going through her head, Maggie thought that sleep would never come, but gradually her racing mind became quieter. It had all been such a long time ago, and nothing she could do or say would change anything now. She drifted off eventually but was then troubled by dreams in which she, herself, was drowning – floundering up and down in deep water. Her eyes were streaming, and she was blinded by the running water, only the difference in light levels enabled her to know whether she was above or below the surface. In her dream she had learnt a few strokes of breaststroke but was by no means a swimmer. As she rose and sank again a voice came in her head "Swim you idiot!". She had no idea where the voice came from, was it her own sense of self-preservation or was it her guardian angel, if she did in fact have one? The shock of the voice in her head made her regain control of her senses, and her limbs, and she struck out with her arms, reaching towards the light.

Maggie opened her eyes with a shock and saw daylight flooding into her bedroom. Morning had come at last.

CHAPTER THREE

At 9.15 next morning Maggie strapped her grand-daughter into the car seat in the rear of the Suzuki. Every Tuesday and Thursday she would drive Emily the five miles down to her Welsh language playgroup, which was based in a hall on the same site as the school where her daughter-in-law Catrin taught. Catrin had to leave earlier to get to work, as the primary school lessons started at 9 am, and Maggie enjoyed having one-to-one time with Emily. The journeys there and back (she would return to collect her at 12.00), though short, were quite a highlight of her day. On this morning, they arrived early as the traffic had been light and the weather conditions fine, at least for the moment. The sky was darkly overcast but as yet no rain had fallen.

She parked up in the carpark and then went to sit in the back with Emily until it was time for the doors to open at 9.45.

"You will be going to big school in September," she told her. "Are you looking forward to it? You will be able to go in with Mummy every day."

"Yes, but Mam won't be teaching me to start with. She has already told me I will be in the baby class so I will have a different teacher. But I still think I will like it. I will know a lot of the children in the baby class from playgroup."

"Do you have any special friends?"

"Yes, I mostly play with Emma and Ani."

"What about Hari from next door? He is the same age as you."

"Oh, he doesn't play with me at playgroup. He plays with the boys."

"So, who is your favourite then?"

"My favourite of all of them, or just playgroup?"

"All of them," Maggie laughed, as if Emily were talking about hundreds of friends.

"Well, my really special friend is Trissi."

"And where does Trissi live, lovey?"

"Silly Nana," Emily looked up at her through those large, grey-blue eyes that reminded her so much of Steve and smiled. "Trissi lives with us, of course."

* * * * *

Maggie parked the Suzuki outside the general shop in the village and popped in to pick up the papers. She was still pondering whether to tell Catrin and Sam what Emily had said about Trissi. They were already concerned, she knew. Emily had been talking about her invisible friend for a while and Sam was quite worried about it. Maggie felt a sudden rush of love for her granddaughter. She was a sweet, affectionate little thing, more like Sam than Catrin, she felt. She liked her daughter-in-law but thought there were a few sharp edges to her personality. "She's certainly nobody's fool," she thought to herself, and perhaps it was just as well for Sam was almost too good-natured. Maggie feared he would be easy to take advantage of, but hopefully Catrin would make sure that did not happen.

As Maggie left the shop, newspapers, and a carton of milk in hand, she met the postman.

"Hi Roy, how are you? Any mail for us?"

"Here you are Maggie – two for the business, and a private one for you."

She sometimes thought the postman was a bit too interested in his job, verging on being nosy almost, but he was good-natured and friendly, and it was difficult to take exception to his comments.

She glanced quickly at the mail before slipping it under her arm as she opened the Suzuki door. He was right, she thought. Two printed envelopes addressed to Nant-y-felin, and a handwritten letter for her.

Arriving back at her kitchen, she put the kettle on to boil while opening the handwritten envelope. The other two letters she would pop down to the office later.

She thought she had recognised the handwriting and she was right. Her cousin Sylvie's daughter was getting married in October and the letter enclosed invitations for her, Sam and Catrin.

"It's only a small wedding," Sylvie had written, "Caroline doesn't want a lot of fuss, so we are not able to ask the children, just the adults.

"It will be lovely to see you again, we haven't met face to face since Ellie's funeral," Sylvie had continued, "where have all the years gone? I find it hard to think about Sam all grown up, even though you've sent me photos."

Maggie suddenly felt overwhelmed with a fresh wave of grief. How strange that she should have had this letter the morning after her dream. It was true, though, she and Sylvie had not met face to face in all that time.

As she was still considering her letter and how they would reply, the telephone rang.

"Hello Mrs Johnson? it's the Ward Sister from Ward A15 at the Royal Shrewsbury Hospital."

Maggie's heart was in her mouth – who was in trouble? She did a quick head count – Sam was working outside, Catrin was teaching, and she had only just dropped little Emily off at nursery school.

"Yes?" she answered breathlessly.

"We admitted a lady via A&E last night. She is very confused, but we found a letter in her pocket which you had sent her. There did not seem to be any contact details for anyone else. Perhaps you could tell us a bit about her, or come in to see her and clear up a few things?"

"Well, yes, of course. I will help in any way I can. Is it..." her mind was racing, "Is it Opal? Opal Graham?"

"That was the name she gave us, although she had suffered concussion and was very confused. She had been in an accident at home, fell down the stairs she said. She doesn't appear to be badly hurt, apart from a lot of bruising, but we need to keep her in for a day or so, due to the concussion."

"I see ... well I will certainly come in to see her – I'll pack a bag with a few things too."

"That would be extremely helpful, Mrs Johnson. We will see you later and explain everything in more detail. Is there anyone else we should inform in the meantime?"

"I'm not sure – I have not seen her for many years and, even then, I did not know her very well. If I think of anyone I will ring back, but I doubt I can tell you anything else now."

Maggie put the phone down more confused than ever. Opal had written to her a few months back saying she was planning to come and stay in the area and would like to see her but would prefer not to stay at the Mill complex itself. Maggie had written back giving the addresses of some holiday cottages that were available to rent but had heard nothing further from her. She certainly did not know that Opal had arrived in the area.

*****

"Can you manage a cup of tea, love?"

Opal fought through the mists that still seemed to be swimming around her eyes. "Yes … yes that would be nice. Thank you."

The smiling ward orderly placed a cup on the trolley by her bed, and then moved on rapidly. So many patients and so little time.

Opal tried, cautiously, to sit up and after waiting for her head to clear a little, gradually reached out towards the comforting drink. She felt less woozy now, but her head was throbbing and her whole body ached.

A vigilant nurse was instantly at her side.

"Mrs Graham – good to see you awake now. How are you this morning?"

"Oh, well, I am not sure. Everything seems to be hurting and I have a terrible headache."

"That's hardly surprising," the nurse was professionally sympathetic, "You had a very nasty fall. I'll bring you some pain relief – that should help."

Was it a fall? Opal could not make up her mind – had she fallen or had Paul really pushed her? They had certainly tussled at the head of the staircase. The holiday cottage had an upside-down layout with the sitting room on the first floor to take account of the view of the mountains, so that was where she had received her visitor the previous evening.

Between sips of revitalising tea, she tried to make sense of events in the past that may have led to last night's incident.

She gradually became aware that her career, which had shown so much promise in her early 20's, had been destroyed by the circumstances surrounding Ellie's death. Somehow as a result, she had become frightened of living, fearful of relationships and had retreated to the safety of her inner life.

Opal had music in her blood. Her father had been a musician in a Jamaican steel band which came over to England on tour. Her mother Sophie, a student at teacher training college, had met him in Edgbaston after one of his gigs, and been bowled over by his easy charm and good humour. They had dated for several months and she had felt they had a lasting relationship. It was only after the band had returned to Jamaica that Sophie had discovered she was pregnant. There was no way she would have given up the baby. She wrote to tell Wesley, who offered financial help but told her he would not be able to come back to England.

After a while, the financial contributions dried up and she lost contact with Wesley completely. Sophie threw herself on the compassion of her mother and father while she completed her teacher training and later managed to get a job as a music teacher at a private school in Worcestershire. Opal's father did have one major input into her life, however. He had written to Sophie when she first told him the news:

"One thing, sweetheart – if the babe is a girl you must call her Opal – she will be serene and glowing on the outside, but her heart will burn like fire."

Sophie had told Opal the story of her birth while she was still in her early teens. Now as she looked back at what her life had become after Ellie, she felt sad.

It was a long, long time since she had allowed her heart to burn like fire.

Suddenly she looked down for the pendant she had always worn around her neck. It was not there, and her heart sank, but as she put down her teacup, she saw it on top of the little cupboard by the side of the hospital bed.

It was a precious opal, milky pale on the surface but burning with fire in blue, red and orange flashes at its heart, and she had always loved it.

When she was 16, her father had made a brief appearance back in her life. He was over in England on another steel band tour and had contacted her mother. He wanted to get in touch with Opal again. Her mother had had many reservations.

"He is not reliable, Opal. If you do meet up with him, he will probably only let you down. I don't want you to have to cope with the disappointment and heartbreak I had when he left me to cope on my own."

"It's okay, Mum," Opal had fearlessly replied. She had been quite feisty in those days, she recalled. Her mother and stepfather had done everything they could to make her childhood safe and secure, and to guard her from any unpleasantness about her mixed-race heritage.

After Sophie had worked for a few years at the school, the headmaster had been widowed, and Sophie had helped him through his grief. Within 18 months he had asked her to marry him and together they had done their best to make Opal feel loved and supported.

To Sophie's sorrow there had been no further children, no half-brothers or sisters, and Opal had grown up an only child but knew in her heart that her mother and step-father were by far the best parents she could have asked for.

"I won't let my heart be broken by my birth Dad." She reassured her mother. "I would like to see him though, I'm curious. He does make up half of my genes after all."

Her mother laughed. "Well don't say I didn't warn you."

So she did meet up with her birth father and, as her mother had warned her, he had not stayed around for long. After he returned to the West Indies, she had never heard from him again. He had still been in England for her seventeenth birthday though, and on that day, he had presented her with the pendant.

It must have cost quite of lot of his tour earnings, she realised with hindsight, for the chain was 22 carat gold, and the opal large and pulsing with light at its heart. She had loved it immediately. It seemed to suit her character and her approach to life. She wore it like a talisman, and in her early 20's had felt the world was at her feet, especially after Steve had asked her to work with him in his music studio at the Mill, and to go touring in Europe. But its luck had failed her, as her father had, and now it only served to remind her of what she had lost all those years before.

The nurse returned with some medication and a glass of water.

"I've brought you some painkillers which should help. They are only mild ones to start with. If you feel uncomfortable, I can ask the doctor to give you something stronger. By the way, there is a visitor waiting to see you. I don't know whether you feel up to it?"

"Who ... who is it?" Opal still felt really confused.

"A lady called Maggie Johnson – she helped to identify you when you were admitted on to the ward."

Opal sighed with relief – at least the person waiting to see her was not ... the person she now most feared.

"Oh Maggie, thank you so much for coming," Opal had tears of relief in her eyes. Finally, someone to talk to who might understand what she had been through.

"How are you feeling Opal? It was such a shock to hear what had happened. Did you fall? The ward sister did not seem to know."

Maggie was shocked to see how much Opal had changed, although she knew this was inevitable in view of the years that had passed. Opal's honey-coloured skin was still smooth and relatively unlined, but her once bouncy, tight black curls were now liberally streaked with grey, and lay dishevelled on the pillow. A bandage covered one side of her head and she looked much smaller than Maggie remembered, as if all the life and fire had been sucked out of her, leaving her frail and empty.

"I am still trying to make sense of what happened myself," Opal admitted. "I had booked one of the holiday cottages that you told me about – Ty Glas, on the outskirts of the village. I was going to ring you the day after I arrived, when I had settled in properly, but in the evening, I had a visitor ..."

"A visitor? Who beside me knew you were coming?"

"Paul. I had written to him at the same time I wrote to you. What happened all those years ago has been really playing on my mind lately. I had a cancer scare – I'm okay now," she added hastily seeing Maggie's concern. "But it made me want to come to terms with the past and let you know what I did not say at the time."

"You know that Paul and I are divorced? We have been for many years now ..."

"Yes, he did mention it – I wrote to both of you separately at the Mill. If you did not see the letter for Paul, someone else must have forwarded Paul's letter to his new address."

"Sam, probably," Maggie interjected, "he still has a lot of contact with Paul."

"Anyway, he had been in touch by phone to find out exactly when I was arriving, and he came to see me last night.

I think he wanted to talk to me before I had a chance to speak to anyone else. He wanted me to keep quiet about his conversation with Ellie the day before she died.

"I don't know how well you know Ty Glas, but it has been built into the hillside and the front door access leads into the living area on the first floor to make the most of the views, with the bedrooms on the floor underneath. I let him in, and we chatted for a while but then, when I said I wanted to clear up all the mystery and misunderstandings of the past, we argued. He did not want me to tell you, or anyone else, what he had told me after Ellie died. I said I needed to get it all out of my system so I could finally move on with my life and that was when he really lost it somehow. By then I was standing at the top of the stairs leading down to the bedrooms and he roughly pushed past me on his way out. I ended up in a heap at the bottom of the stairs."

"Do you think he meant to push you?"

"No, not really – well, I can't say I am sure either way. He must have been concerned about me though because he is the only one who could have called the ambulance. I was barely conscious when they arrived and brought me here. But I always knew he had a temper."

"Yes, me too," Maggie shivered. "That was why we finally broke up. Things had never been brilliant right from the start of our marriage. I always had to watch every word I said and then finally it all got too much for me. But what was he so worried about you telling us?"

"You know he always had a 'thing' about Ellie?"

"I had noticed," Maggie's tone was sardonic.

"After that terrible day when the police came to tell us what had happened, he was dreadfully upset. He came into my room that night. We were both so shocked and trying to console each other. He said he had told Ellie the day before that Steve and I were going to go on tour together and would not be coming back but going off together for good. I think he wanted Ellie to turn to him for comfort – he never dreamt what would happen. It was all a complete lie of course. Steve and I had been working together in the studio at the Mill, but it was never anything other than a working relationship."

"Do you think that what Paul told her was the reason Ellie did what she did?"

"I think it was the final straw. She felt she had no one left to talk to, and no other options available."

"But why take little Tristan with her? He was only three years old. That was so cruel, and heart-breaking for the rest of us."

"I have spent a long time thinking about that over the years. I do not think she saw it as cruel. All she could see was that the world was full of danger and it was her way of keeping him safe from harm and emotional pain. She could not bear to go on living, but she could not bear to leave him behind to suffer either.

"There was one other thing, Maggie, but it's very awkward..." Opal hesitated, and then continued, "he said he had told Ellie that night that he had doubts about being Sam's father."

Opal looked up at Maggie apprehensively, afraid of giving more pain.

"What exactly did he tell Ellie?" Maggie asked anxiously.

"He said he thought Steve was Sam's father. He told her that you and Steve had been close while she was in hospital after her previous suicide attempt several months before Sam was born."

Maggie looked devastated. "I had no idea he even suspected – I would have done anything to prevent Ellie hearing that. But it is true – I was trying to comfort Steve when he was so upset about the suicide attempt, and it just happened, somehow. I was always so fond of Steve. It broke my heart to see him in bits after Ellie tried to kill herself.

"It was only the one time – I felt so guilty afterwards for betraying Ellie – but that was enough, and I found I was pregnant a few weeks afterwards. I tried to pretend, even to myself, that the baby was Paul's, but he must have seen through this. Although to be fair he always treated Sam like his own son, whatever his suspicions might have been."

After Maggie had left the ward, Opal found herself reliving those final weeks with Steve. Although she had told Maggie the truth when she said there had been nothing between them when Ellie died, she had always been very attracted to him. His easy-going charm, and boyish good looks were difficult to resist. She had hoped that if she could help him through the devastation of losing both Ellie and his little boy, there might eventually be a chance of a real relationship between them. That was until that dreadful day when she went with him to Chester, the events of which had made him decide to leave behind all the grief and trauma and cross the Atlantic.

Once he had left for America, Opal saw no point in staying on and went back to the safety of her home in Worcestershire, choosing a dull, uneventful life over the chance of the passion she had once embraced. She had followed her mother in taking a teacher-training degree and diverted her love of music into teaching it to other people, instead of living it herself.

In her thirties she had married a rather boring, but reliable, accountant, but he did not want children, and gradually they drifted apart, leading lives more and more separate, until he found love with a clerk in his office and they divorced. After that, she had thrown herself into her teaching and lived life at second-hand through the efforts of her students, the more promising of whose careers she followed with great delight.

In the last few years, she had been very conscious of the passage of time. The cancer scare had made her re-evaluate her life. Maybe there was still time, she thought. Her cancer diagnosis had taught her that every single day mattered, and should be filled with joy and hope, not spent in recriminations and regrets. If all of those who had witnessed the events that had happened so long ago could put them firmly behind them now, maybe there could be a new start, a new hope for the ones that survived.

Chapter Four

As he strolled down the country lane in the cool sunlight, listening to the plaintive bleating of the lambs in the surrounding fields and the deeper responses from their mothers, Mike could not help thinking how lucky he was to have returned to this place. It really did feel like coming home, somehow, even though he had been born many miles away.

Mid Wales always looked at its best in spring, with the new green growth in the hedgerows, and the daffodils and primroses on the roadside verges glowing golden in the sunshine. He had seen the house he had so recently bought advertised purely by chance, just when he was thinking he should start making plans for the future. He had been alone for three years now, it was time he began living again.

Those years in Birmingham, imperative at the time, had drained him and it was a delight to enjoy the countryside of Montgomeryshire once again.

Janey was never far from his thoughts. The first year after her death had been the hardest but even now, he would think of something he wanted to share with her and have a sudden rush of renewed grief and loneliness. He had not been sure if he was doing the right thing moving back to Wales, but he felt it might help him to move on and get on with his life.

He had forgotten how much he had loved this part of the world when they had moved here originally from Manchester. He and Janey had met while teaching at a comprehensive in Salford and had married and bought a small house in Worsley. After a few years teaching history, he had taken on a role as student counsellor while at the school and had decided he much preferred one to one contact to trying to get the best out of large classes of mixed ability children, some of whom could not comprehend the relevance of history to their own lives. He therefore decided to retrain as a psychotherapist.

After he completed his training, they had seen a vacancy for a counsellor advertised at a GP practice in Montgomeryshire. Janey had been supportive. She had been becoming increasing tired while teaching, and now it seemed likely that had been a symptom of the cancer that had yet to be diagnosed. They both looked forward enthusiastically to their new, less stressful, life in mid Wales.

They had sold their house in Worsley and decided to rent once Mike's job offer was confirmed.

"It will give us time to look around for the perfect 'for-ever' house," Janey told him sensibly.

Sadly, their new beginning had been ruined by Janey's illness within a few months of their decision to move. Her tiredness had grown increasing worse, to the point where Dr Andrew at the surgery had referred her for tests. The appointments came back so quickly that they were forewarned that it was something serious. Normally there was a wait of several months for routine cases.

Mike felt even sadder that they had put off the decision to start a family.

"There's still plenty of time, Mike," Janey had told him when they moved. "Let's wait until we are settled in our own house before we think about babies."

But there was not plenty of time. During Janey's treatment in Birmingham she was far too ill to think about having children. Afterwards, although the treatment had prolonged her life by many years, he did not feel she had the stamina to cope with small children, and the specialists had said her treatment would affect her ability to conceive. They had decided, between them, to concentrate on each other and Mike had felt that Janey's recovery and recuperation were his top priority.

The sound of the brook rushing past him at the roadside turned his thoughts back to his interaction with Ellie all those years before. At that time, the combination of his wife's illness and what he felt had been his mishandling of the sessions with Ellie, had seemed like the end of his world.

He remembered his last meeting with Dr Andrew at the practice and felt guilty that he had left them all so abruptly. He had been almost glad, however, to escape to a different life working at the hospital in Birmingham. He realised that Laurie Andrew had tried to protect him when he had heard the news about Ellie's suicide. Perhaps if he had known immediately it happened, he would have returned straight away to give his input. As it had happened, it was only when Mike rang Laurie to tell him Janey's treatment had finished, that he discovered what Ellie had done on the day of his last meeting with her. He understood that Laurie had been trying to shield him, but he might have felt more comfortable if everything had been brought out into the open in time for the post-mortem. As it was, by the time he found out about her death, it was too late to make any difference to the outcome, and he had not wanted to reopen wounds that might gradually have been healing.

Although Janey's treatment had finished and she was regarded as 'cured', her health had never really recovered and they had decided to remain in the Birmingham area, close to the hospital, in case she needed further treatment. The house they had once planned to buy in Montgomeryshire was purchased in Bromsgrove instead.

Since Janey's death however he had come to realise that this was where his heart really lay – out in the gentle hills and quiet lanes, where the sound of bleating sheep in the fields, and birdsong in the hedgerows, drowned out the hum of traffic on the main tourist route in the distance.

Suddenly Mike realised that his supposedly un-planned ramble had taken him to the Old Mill. Ellie had told him all about the mill she and her sister had inher-ited during his sessions with him, but it was a shock to suddenly see it in front of him, when he had no con-scious idea of heading this way. The mountain loom-ed up at the back behind the yard, but this was the sunny side of the valley and it did not feel threatening in any way.

The overnight rain had cleared leaving everywhere fresh and fragrant. The mountain, once badly scarred from the earlier quarrying, was greening over nicely now, he noticed. It was far greener than when he had lived here before. Nature had a way of reclaiming the land that man had no further use for.

As his gaze moved upwards, he saw small white puffs of cloud chasing each other over the top, like young lambs playing 'King of the Castle', and he heard the mew of buzzards circling overhead. It was strangely quiet for an April day, he thought – not even the hum of a distant tractor working the fields.

He noticed the stylish new slate sign at the gate that read "Nant-y-felin". From the Welsh that he had picked up he knew this literally meant "the Mill Stream". He guessed they had changed the name to distinguish it from many other repurposed watermills, which were abundant in Montgomeryshire. The yard was empty of vehicles and looked deserted. Perhaps they had all gone off to Oswestry – it was market day, he remembered.

He had heard all about the Mill since he moved back from the locals in the village. They still called it the Old Mill and could tell various, and conflicting, tales about its past.

As someone who had always had a strong interest in social history, he felt it sad that there were so few remaining working mills. He recognised, however, that there was only work for a few artisan millers in the modern world. Besides which, he realised, the cost of replacing all the working machinery, and making changes to the waterflow would in this case have been prohibitive.

He was impressed with the work they had done, keeping the original buildings as authentic as possible, but making the whole site attractive and workable. Even from the road he could see the flower troughs bright with violas in yellows and purples. The site where he guessed the mill pond had once been, had been filled in, turfed over, and planted with a flowering cherry which was just reaching its best.

As he stood, hesitating, outside the Mill entrance, the hazy sunlight glinted on a shard of broken glass that lay in the middle of the lane. He bent to pick it up, worried in case it shredded someone's tyres as they drove though, and a sudden memory came to him. After his second meeting with Ellie he had had a very vivid dream. He had taken a crystal decanter into the kitchen to wash before refilling it. As he held it up to the light, admiring its delicate, faceted fragility, it had suddenly slipped through his wet fingers, smashing into a thousand pieces on the flags of the kitchen floor. In the dream, he had bent to sweep up the fragments and a shard had pierced his finger, causing large drops of blood to fall over the kitchen worktops as he reached hastily for a cloth to stop the bleeding. As he wrapped his wound, he noticed the sugar bowl standing by the kettle. Thick red drops had fallen into it and showed up starkly against the white crystalline sugar. It was such a vivid image it had stayed with him to return intermittently over the years. With hindsight, he could have interpreted this dream as a warning of some kind, he thought, but at the time he had just stored it away in the back of his mind. Perhaps it was all part of the past that needed to be confronted.

His feelings at the Mill entrance only served to make him more aware that he had to face up to what had had happened with Ellie and acknowledge his part in the events that followed. He had initially fought against thinking about it too much. It was too painful, especially as he had been coping with Janey's illness at the same time.

One thing the experience had taught him was that one to one counselling of the kind he had been doing was no longer a role he was comfortable with. Instead his work at the hospital had involved helping patients with cancer, and their relatives, come to terms with their diagnoses and the effects of their various treatments.

That work was demanding, and sometimes heartbreaking, but not open to the dangers of misunderstanding in the intense and dangerous way that had occurred with Ellie.

He felt now that if he could come to terms with Ellie's suicide, he would be able to find true peace in this location, to which he had been longing to return.

He considered walking through the gate and up to the Mill complex. He had heard that Ellie's sister was still living at the property, but felt it would be too awkward to suddenly announce himself out of the blue: "Hello, I'm the counsellor your sister was seeing when she killed herself" – not really the best kind of introduction.

Just as well, perhaps, that the yard did look deserted or he might have attempted it, although he knew it would have been a bad idea to approach strangers in such a way. He had heard a lot about the family from Ellie, about her sister Maggie in particular, but had never met any of them. He would wait and give it time. If he were meant to get in touch with Ellie's family, then he was sure an opportunity would present itself.

He decided to carry on with his walk down the lane that led from the Mill back to the village, reflecting as he walked on about his return to this part of the world.

The area had hardly changed during the years he had been away. More traffic on the main roads perhaps, and a few small housing estates on the edges of the local villages and towns, but the verdant, sheep-cropped hills remained the same as he remembered, and the lanes and farm-tracks still called out to him for exploration. He enjoyed his solitary rambles through muddy, leaf-strewn woods and up into the hill-tops.

He had bought a property three miles from the nearest village – a small, detached cottage that had been rented out as a holiday home for many years. It had been a farmworker's cottage originally, he guessed, and had been built centuries ago of the local grey stone. The roof slates must have come from the old quarry originally, and when he was replacing the few that had slipped off and broken, he had to source them from a reclamation yard to make sure they were still in keeping with the original building. It was not listed, unlike many of the more important old houses in the area, but he still felt it would be sacrilege to use the cheaper, imported slates which now featured on most of the new builds in the region.

He had used a bridging loan to buy the property and renovate it while he was still living in Bromsgrove. He would come up for days at a time to do the work but did not move in properly until the end of March. He wanted to make sure the house was watertight and comfortable before he made it his permanent home. Now he was beginning to think that this was where he could settle and really belong.

If he could reconcile his feelings about Ellie, perhaps he could learn to really enjoy his life here. He had tentatively put the Bromsgrove house on the market but would not rush to sell it until he knew he could really settle back in this area.

His walk had brought him almost back to his cottage now and he was hailed as he passed the neighbouring property.

"Dr Lane! How are you today? I wonder if I could have a word?"

His neighbour, Dorothy Ellis, had opened a downstairs window, the cool sunlight glinting on her gold framed glasses as she called out to him.

"Can you spare a moment now, I wonder. I have coffee and some home-made scones on the go?"

Mike smiled warmly. He was growing fond of Dorothy, a woman he guessed to be in her mid 70's, but who was still active in the community.

"I never say no to your home-made scones," he laughed as he entered through the front door. He had only been in the cottage two or three times before but already felt very at home there and enjoyed Dorothy's motherly fussing. She did remind him of his own mother, who had died a few years before he lost Janey.

He loved her old-fashioned kitchen. There was no run of machine-made units but antique stand-alone solid wood cabinets in dark oak, a comforting Rayburn warming the area and a wooden settle smothered in multi-coloured cushions along one wall. In the centre of the room was a scrubbed pine-topped table with four wheelback chairs placed around it, and there were bright red gingham curtains hanging from the window which overlooked the lane. He knew from a previous visit that the modern necessities of washing machine and fridge were tucked away in the adjoining walk-in larder, but the kitchen felt so comforting and homely he always stayed longer than he intended.

"I've just walked past Nant-y-felin," he decided to tell her. "It looks an interesting place - do you know anything about its history?"

Dorothy put some scones carefully in front of him, as if weighing up in her mind what to tell him.

"It's an unhappy house," she began, "some local people say its cursed, although there has been nothing in the last few years to give it that name. Twenty or so years ago a young woman who lived there was tragically drowned with her young son. There were rumours that she did it deliberately, but the official version was a dreadful accident. People always talk though, whether there is any truth in the gossip or not. It does seem an unfortunate place. The people who had it before the current owners would not live there. I knew them a little – Gethin and Glenys from Bala way. They had inherited the run-down site from a relative and had planned to live there and renovate the old Mill. Such a shame when these old buildings fall into neglect and ruin," she paused to pour them both a cup of tea.

"Anyway, they stayed there for a few weeks and then left suddenly. Apparently, Glenys refused to live there – she said she kept hearing someone crying in the night. Not long after their house in Bala caught fire and they were both killed. I suppose that must have been how the people who live there now came to have it. So, you can see how bad things came to be associated with it."

Mike was silent for a while, taking in what she had told him.

"What do you know about the people who live there now?"

"I know Maggie, she's treasurer of the Flower Show committee – Maggie Johnson. She runs the place with her son and his wife. They seem genuinely nice people – anxious to fit in without being too pushy. They have been here long enough now to be part of the community

– and the tragedy with her sister and the child gained them a great deal of support in the village. That reminds me ....." She changed the subject, wanting to move on to less distressing topics. "I am going to put the arm on you now," Dorothy threatened, with a broad grin, as she offered him yet another scone. "We need some help with the village flower show – there are always plenty of people keen to enter with local produce but finding people for the committee is always hard. Would you be prepared to consider it?"

Mike hesitated. "Well, I am so new to living here. Would people not resent it if I started pushing in?"

"No, no," Dorothy reassured him. "People are quick to moan, I agree, but it is so hard to get anyone to commit to doing any kind of work. We used to have quite a lot of farmer's wives on the committee, but they all have jobs of their own now, they are no longer content to just stay on the farms, and then they all say they haven't got the time."

"Well, I'm prepared to come along to some of the meetings if you like – I would not have to commit straight away, would I?"

"Certainly not, and it would be a way of making more friends in the area."

Mike had taken early retirement but did not rule out finding either voluntary or paid part-time work in the area. He was in no rush though – plenty of time to make sure everything was working out the way he wanted it to. Sometimes though, planning too much could get in the way. It was good to have a spontaneous reaction and let life take him where it would.

CHAPTER FIVE

The change in Opal had shocked Maggie, although she realised that no-one would have looked their best in a hospital bed. The trauma of the accident alone would account for the pinched aspect to her features and the haunted look in her eyes.

She wondered how Opal felt on seeing her again. Maggie's pride had made her determined not to let herself go, but she surely looked quite different from the Maggie Opal would have remembered. Her hair was no longer auburn but coloured a soft beige blonde, and despite trying to keep an eye on her weight, she was no longer the neat size 12 she had been when they first moved up to Montgomeryshire, but now a more matronly 16. She suddenly became aware of how much time had passed since they last met. The years had melted into each other somehow, only Sam's progression from child to adult, to becoming a parent himself, marking the passing of time to her in any meaningful way.

Sometimes, looking back, she felt that she had spent a lot of those years hiding in a dark tunnel of depression, trying to come to terms with loss and guilt, and hiding away like an injured animal until the pain had slowly eased a little but never really left her.

She drove back from the hospital with her head in a whirl. At first she could hardly believe what Opal had told her, but she knew from first-hand what Paul could be like, manipulative and controlling, and she had been on the wrong end of his fist on two occasions, even if they were years apart.

She remembered their last row, many years before, when she had finally found the courage to stand up to him and had ended up in a heap on the kitchen floor.

He had wanted her to give up her part-time job at the vets and spend all her time at the Mill. He had always tried to control her, knock her confidence, keep her docile.

"I won't give up my job, Paul. Its only two days a week after all, I can still do my work here as well. Sam is at school most of the time so there is plenty of time to fit everything in."

"I don't want you out there, mixing with who knows who. I want to know where you are and what you are doing."

"Why don't you trust me, Paul? You've never said any of this before."

"Well, I'm saying it now – I want you to give up that job and keep away from those people."

"No, Paul. I am not going to. Those people, you call them, they are my friends. Heaven knows I need some friends after everything that has happened here."

Her point-blank refusal had been the trigger, and he had lost control and knocked her to the ground.

That was it! He would never hit her again or try to control her. She had taken her bruises to the local medical centre, and reported him to the police, only agreeing not to press charges if he kept at a safe distance in future. They had maintained a civil relationship in front of Sam, and their neighbours, but there was no way Maggie would ever let him back into her affections.

In the years that followed her divorce, she had tried to form other relationships, but her heart and mind were still too full of grief and guilt over Ellie, and she could not find it in herself to let anyone else in.

There would be no chance of rekindling any relationship with Steve, even if he did return from America. He had been her first love, but through the intervening years she could see that they were not compatible in any way. She had fallen for him when she was still extremely young, but she knew now that he had never really grown up at all, was still a child inside. He was unable to face up to things, would rather run away, as he had done after Ellie's death. She knew she had to take her share of the blame for what had happened but, if he had behaved differently, things might have had a better outcome.

Jeremy, the solicitor for the vet's practice who had helped with her divorce, had started showing a romantic interest in her after she ceased to be his client, but although she made it clear she was very grateful for his help, she gently let him know that she was not ready for another relationship.

In later years, she had become friendly with Catrin's Dad, Huw, especially after Sam and Catrin married, but somehow she felt there was too many family ties between them for a chance of any kind of relationship other than friendship. Besides, his sister Delyth was so firmly entrenched in the family set-up as a substitute mother for Catrin, that Maggie did not think there was really room for anyone else.

* * * * *

By the time Maggie returned to the Mill on that April afternoon it was after five o'clock. At the hospital she had visited the League of Friends shop to buy some bits and pieces to make Opal more comfortable and stayed with her until the end of afternoon visiting.

She enjoyed driving back through the lanes: she always felt mid-Wales looked at its prettiest in April. She was not keen on the busy A5, but once she had turned off towards Welshpool, she always knew she was coming home, and felt comforted by the tranquil scenery. She loved this part of the world so much. Ever since the first visit when she, Ellie, Steve, and Paul all came to view the property her mother had made over to them, she had felt this was where she belonged.

The soft green hills had seemed familiar to her even then, as if she had known them before, and now she could not bear to be away from them for long. She could not understand the appeal of Snowdonia, so rugged and hostile, when this beautiful area was so often overlooked by those driving through on the way to more dramatic scenery.

She knew Steve and Paul had loved the challenge of the barren rocks and mountains of Snowdonia, but she was far happier in this more comforting landscape.

The Dark Skies project had been mostly her idea, although Steve had a strong interest in astronomy, as well as his commitment to his music with the band. When she had lived on the outskirts of London there had always been the glow of the streetlights, even in the more rural areas, and looking up at the heavens she was far more likely to see the lights of aeroplanes flashing red and white in ghostly silence, than any stars.

As a child, her parents had taken her and Ellie out to the more secret parts of Epping Forest, and it was there she had learnt her love of the countryside and stargazing. Sometimes they would take a tent and camp out overnight, and her father would point out the major constellations like Ursa Major and the W-shaped Cassiopeia, and the stars which made up the Summer Triangle, Vega, Altair and Deneb. He would show her how to trace a line from the Plough to find the pole star. He encouraged her star gazing by buying her star atlases and books about the universe and her place in it. He also bought her bird books and wildlife encyclopaedias, but it was the stars which really called to her heart.

Maggie felt a sudden pang remembering. She had always felt Ellie was his favourite, but now she realised he had spent a lot of time with her, teaching her his passions for wildlife and the countryside. He worked in the City all week but treasured his escapes at the weekend. Now after all these years, she felt the tears welling up as she realised how much she had missed having him in her life. Her mother had been her rock, a solid reliable presence in her life, but her Dad had moulded her soul.

After he died, she had had to be strong, strong for her mother and for Ellie. She felt she had to be the one to keep everything together. She realised that she had let that resolution shape the rest of her life. It was up to her to carry everyone else, and she could not give way to her many doubts and fears, but must just carry on, alone if necessary, holding everything together as well as she could. Sometimes, that burden just felt too heavy to bear.

As Maggie turned into the Mill driveway, she felt proud of what they had achieved.

According to local people in the nearby village, there had been a mill on the site since at least the Middle Ages, and the stone-built property they had taken on had probably been rebuilt and altered through many generations, although any written records about it had perished through fire and flood.

Over the years since they took over the property, they had succeeded in sympathetically renovating the building Maggie's mother had inherited. The mill wheel was no longer operative but preserved as a monument to its past working life. The interior workings had also been retained as far as possible in the large, airy lounge that occupied part of the first floor. This part of the building was now occupied by Sam and Catrin, with a kitchen and utility on the ground floor and bedrooms and bathroom on the second.

Maggie lived in an adjoining part, configured in a similar way over three floors. They had built a new extension to link the original Mill with the neighbouring barn, which was mostly built of smoked glass and wood. Luckily, among Steve's music contacts was a close friend who had trained as an architect before becoming a professional musician. He had drawn up plans for the linking building which had been acceptable to the Planning Department and had charged them a very reasonable price. The extension now functioned as a large central hall and entrance area, and the original barn had been reconfigured into two holiday apartments which brought them a regular income.

They had used the land to the rear of the property for campers, and the odd touring caravan, and renovated some of the smaller outbuildings into dormitory-style accommodation for groups of nature lovers and stargazers.

In the last few years, Steve's former studio building had been converted into an office for Sam to use for his Estate Management work, and somewhere to house the administration for the holiday lets and campsite.

The only project which remained from the original plan was for the former stables at the rear of the complex. As the building at the furthest point from the village, and most free from light-pollution, they had decided this would be the ideal spot for an observatory, and Maggie and Sam were still trying to get together the funds to convert it and buy a top of the range telescope to encourage more serious sky-watchers to come to visit. This was one of the most expensive parts of the business plan and Maggie had not yet had the time, money, or energy to complete it.

"The conversion of the old stable block will have to be for you and Catrin to sort out now," Maggie had told her son.

"I'm exhausted from all the previous work. Its time you and Catrin took over the business full-time. I will still help out with the admin and you can pay me a salary if you wish, but I will make the whole project over to you and Catrin now."

Sam had tried to talk her out of her decision, but she was adamant.

"As long as I still have a home here, I will be quite happy," she reassured him.

Maggie had thrown herself into the project, even more after Ellie's death as she needed something else to think about.

When Maggie and Ellie took over the property, it been neglected for many years. At one time, in the not too distant past, it had been used as a smallholding and pig farm, but the farm buildings had fallen into disrepair over the intervening years. When Maggie's great-uncle had taken it over, it was already in a ruinous state and his plan to renovate it had been cut short when he and his wife were killed in a house fire some miles away from the property.

Maggie had fallen in love with the Mill at first sight. Not so much the building, which was semi-derelict and needed a lot of work, but the location. The Mill was set some yards to the north of a river which ran through a wide, fertile, glacial valley. To the west were the foothills of the Berwyn Mountains, while the English border lay several miles to the east. The south side of the valley was protected by grass-covered hills, which provided shelter from the worst of the wind and weather, and to the north by one of the smaller mountains in the Berwyn range, paths over which led after several miles to the head of the famous Pistyll Rhaeadr waterfall, which could only be accessed by road from the neighbouring valley.

Maggie had only the most tenuous connection with the area. Until she had heard of her mother's inheritance, she had never known there was any connection between her family and this site. She had never been aware the place existed. A family rift had meant her mother had lost touch completely with the uncle who had bequeathed the property, and it was a subject which had never been raised while Maggie was growing up. Somehow, however, she felt that the Mill was in her blood. Its history seemed to call out to her as if she had known it before.

At the time her mother told her the news, Maggie had had enough of London and the suburbs – in her late teens she had loved the commute to London, the excitement of the big City, but in later years she had yearned to get away from the traffic and the noise.

When she, Ellie, Paul, and Steve first came up to look at the place, she was overwhelmed by the emotion she felt. This could be the new start they were all looking for. It could be the glue to hold them together in an exciting new venture, a completely different way of life.

She had wondered even then if her marriage to Paul had been a good idea. It had happened so soon after Ellie and Steve got together, that she wondered if it had been a decision made on the rebound.

She had tried hard to make a go of things but felt the Mill project might bring Paul and herself closer together. Although perhaps the proximity to Steve might not be such a good thing. She tried to put all her doubts aside and concentrate on building up a business that might cement them all together more firmly, rather than pull them apart.

While they were still making up their mind whether to keep the property or put it up for auction, they had booked for the weekend at a B&B in the nearest village. It was early May and there were few visitors about apart from themselves, but the local pub was busy with the caravan owners who came out from the Midlands for the weekends.

They spent the first evening checking out the pub and trying to find out what call there might be for more tourist accommodation in the area.

The pub was painted in traditional black and white with exposed beams, but it was difficult to tell how old it really was as it had been added to and altered over several generations, and must have borne little resemblance to the original building.

The owners Glyn and Norma had only had it for three years and were still putting their own stamp on the business. Norma, the landlady, was serving behind the bar when they arrived, and taking advantage of a lull in customers, Maggie asked her a little more about the village and its potential for tourists and visitors.

"We are still trying to build up a bigger customer base here," Norma had told her. "A lot of people have second-home caravans in the area, and we do a good trade with meals in the summer holidays. Sometimes the husband will bring the family up for a fortnight, go back to work himself, and leave the wife and kids here. If the weather is good, they will stay up all the time, but if it rains, they usually arrange to go back to town fairly quickly."

She filled Maggie in with some background. Glyn was a former BT engineer whose family had lived in the area for many generations. He had had to leave to look for work but when the pub had come up for sale, he and Norma had decided to risk everything they had to fulfil the dream of returning to the area, and bringing up their children in the Welsh countryside.

Maggie was fascinated by their story and hoped that if her family did decide to keep the Mill, there might be a way of working with Glyn and Norma to bring in more customers for both businesses.

There were several caravan sites in the village already, but as these were mainly owner-occupied with people using them as second homes, rather than coming to the area for individual holidays, perhaps there was still plenty of room for the project she, in particular, had in mind.

CHAPTER SIX

On the Saturday of their weekend trip, the two couples had a good look around their new property, trying to decide whether to go ahead with the project or put it on the market and split the cash between them.

Maggie had been by far the keenest on keeping it. The whole place spoke immediately to her heart and she hated the thought that the others might turn it down. Paul was the most doubtful, she felt, and as that thought occurred to her, a wave of dislike for him flooded over her. He obviously knew how much she wanted to keep it, but he was good at finding flaws in everything, including Maggie herself.

"Well, it will be a great deal of work," Paul started in, in his negative way, but before he could say any more Maggie interrupted:

"In its current state it won't fetch very much," she said, as persuasively as she could. "Once we have done some work on it, its value will be greatly increased. We can always put it on the market at any time in the future, if things don't work out, but obviously the more work we have put in, the greater its eventual value will be."

She was desperate that this opportunity should not be lost. She needed them to see what it could mean if they relocated to this new way of life and left all the old hassles behind them. Okay, so things would never be perfect, and their partnership would need as much work as the property, but she really felt it was the answer to so many of their problems.

Finally, she managed to persuade them. They spent the rest of the day working out which jobs needed to be done first.

Maggie pushed her idea for a 'dark skies' project.

It was an ambition she held strongly, and she did not want it to disappear under everyone else's priorities. Once the land was in a tidy condition, they could start having campers, and as the buildings were renovated the project could grow and grow. The bequest had also included some cash which would pay for the initial work at least.

By Saturday night, they had all agreed that they wanted to take the project forward. They could see little use, however, in going back to the property on the Sunday. It would be better to explore its overall position in relation to the rest of Wales, they could then decide how to market their offering once they were ready to do so.

They would also need to research local businesses in the area and get recommendations for local craftsmen to help with the renovations. Glyn and Norma at the pub could probably help them with that. Paul and Steve thought they could do a lot of the hard graft themselves, but they would also need expertise and experience to help them through.

"We can do a lot of research from Chingford – getting quotes and finding local business people by 'phone – we'll come up again in a month's time and see what we can make a start on then."

Steve was taking control now; Maggie was pleased to see. He was almost as keen on the Dark Skies idea as she was, although his main priority was to have a music studio in the new property.

That left the final day of their weekend free to explore the area.

The trip to the coast was Paul's idea.

"We're not that far away – perhaps an hour or so. Let us spend part of the day at the seaside. There's not much more we can do at the Mill for the moment, and we have plenty more time ahead of us."

Maggie was a little disappointed to start with, but maybe they all needed a bit of space to contemplate what they were about to commit to, so she agreed with a good grace.

The weather was disappointing for a day in early May. It was misty on their side of the Berwyns, but once they crossed to the other side, sharp rain blew in on a biting wind.

"That's Wales for you," Steve moaned, as he drove around the sharp bends on the approach to Bala.

"Yes," said Maggie, "but there wouldn't be all this beautiful green grass without the rain."

It was stormy and rough when they reached the coast and pulled up alongside a harbour wall. The sea was wild and fierce, more like a winter scene than a day in May, but they found it exciting and invigorating.

Ellie jumped out of the car and ran over to the harbour steps. The tide was right in and the waves were splashing against the seawall, coming right over onto the road in some places.

Ellie stood enthralled on the top step watching the spray and glorying in the energy of the crashing waves.

"Wait, Ellie, wait," Maggie called out, running after her. "Come away, come away from the edge. One sudden large wave and you will be swept away. It's not safe to be so near."

Ellie looked at her, eyes wild with excitement, and joy in the fury of the storm, but she did allow Maggie to drag her away to a safer viewpoint.

"I love this," she told Maggie. "I love the wildness, the danger, the force of the water."

"Maybe so," said Maggie, "but if it's like this in late spring what must the winters be like?"

"You always have to be so sensible Maggie," her sister shrugged.

* * * * *

A few years later, when Sam and Tristan were toddlers, Maggie and Ellie had returned to the coast on a calm, bucket-and-spade, sandy-beach day, and found a small empty bay between Barmouth and Harlech. As the two small children sat happily digging into the freshly washed sand and playing with shells, Maggie turned to her sister.

"Do you remember the first time we came to the seaside near here?"

"Oh yes, you wouldn't believe it was the same stretch of coast, would you?" Ellie laughed. "But I did enjoy it – the power of the water and the wind, even if it was a bit frightening."

"Perhaps it was the fear you enjoyed the most," Maggie suggested.

"Maybe. Sometimes it is good to feel the power of the elements, it can make you feel more alive. It makes you realise how helpless we really are against the forces of nature. When you really think about it, we are all on an exceptionally fine line of survival – if the sun were a few degrees hotter, or a few degrees colder we would none of us be here at all."

Maggie felt surprised to hear her sister voicing such an insight, but then immediately felt guilty. She sometimes underestimated Ellie, and thought she was only interested in herself and her own immediate concerns.

Chapter Seven

"Hi Mum!"

Sam was waiting for Maggie when she drove into the Mill yard and called to her through the open window of the Suzuki. He had seen her briefly before she left, and she had phoned him from the hospital to let him know what was going on, but he was still puzzled.

Sam had only been four or five when Ellie and Tristan died. He did not think he could remember them or his uncle Steve, who had gone to live in America soon after the tragedy. Sam and his mother and father had continued to live at the Mill but, during his early teenage years, his parents had split up and Paul had moved out. As far as he could tell his dad had relinquished any claim to the property when he left and his mother had made enough from renting out the holiday lets and her part-time job with the local vets to keep the two of them. It had not really occurred to him before, but it must have been quite a struggle for her, alone with just a teenage boy for company and support.

When Sam left college, he got a job as a trainee Land Agent with an Oswestry firm of Estate Agents. After qualifying he had become the manager of various farms and small estates nearby. Now he and his wife, Catrin, and four-year-old daughter Emily, had taken over the part of the property formerly occupied by Steve and Ellie, with Maggie still living in her original accommodation.

The small storage building that Steve had originally converted into a recording studio had been reconfigured as an estate office, from which Sam ran his business with administrative help from his mother and Catrin, when she had time off from her teaching duties at the local primary school.

His ambition now was to complete the original 'Dark Skies' idea first conceived by his mother, by converting the one remaining semi-derelict building into a proper under-cover observatory and lecture room where they could host seminars and special interest holidays for star-gazing enthusiasts. They had already had visitors longing to escape from the light-pollution of the cities, and full of enthusiasm for the star-studded vistas they could offer. The additional facilities would complement that interest and enhance their reputation as a special interest destination.

He had sounded out Glyn and Norma at the village pub to see if they were interested in putting up any visitors they might not themselves have room for, but there was still a great deal of work to do.

He watched as his mother parked the Suzuki outside the main building, and got out of the vehicle, grabbing her bag from the passenger seat.

"How was the visit then, Mum?"

"It's a wonder I got home in one piece," his mother told him. "My mind was so full of what I learned from Opal."

"What happened then, Mum? You told me before you went that she had had a fall ... "

Sam looked at his mother with concern. She looked tired and anxious, emotionally exhausted. Suddenly he became aware of the passing years and realised with a shock that his mother was no longer a young woman. She had tried to look after herself and could probably pass for much younger than she really was, but the years were beginning to tell now, he thought. Perhaps the shock of Opal's sudden arrival had brought back all the trauma from that time, so many years before, when his mother's only sister, and his cousin Tristan had drowned.

"Yes, well it turns out it was not a fall. Someone pushed her…"

"Pushed her – who on earth would do something like that?"

"Well, I hate to tell you, but she says it was Paul,"

"Dad? Why on earth would Dad do something like that?"

"Heaven knows, Sam. It has been many years since I tried to understand what was going on in Paul's head. We've been apart for many years now so I can't really expect to know what drives him."

"But what happened exactly? What does she say?"

"Apparently she asked to see him when she arrived here last week. She said there was something she wanted to clear up with us all. Something we should all know – in connection with your Aunt Ellie."

Sam was even more confused. He knew Ellie had died many years before and his cousin Tristan, who was three years old, had died at the same time, but he had never heard the full details. He had really preferred not to think about it as he grew older, it had just seemed such a terrible time in everyone's life.

"I think it's time you knew the whole story," Maggie stroked his hair, just as she had done when he was a child. "It's something your father-in-law can fill you in with, he was an eye-witness to what happened."

"Huw?" Sam was even more confused, "Why was he involved? You never mentioned him before?"

"I know, love," his mother looked anxious, "there were many things we tried to keep from you when you were younger, but now the time has come for us all to face up to what happened. We have tried to hide it away for too long and it needs to come out into the daylight. I think that is what brought Opal here."

As she, Sam and Catrin sat together sharing a hasty supper, Maggie suddenly remembered her letter.

"I've heard from Cousin Sylvie today," she pulled the letter from the pocket she had hastily put it in when the telephone rang that morning.

"Her daughter is getting married in the autumn and there are invitations for me, and you two, but you would not be able to take Emily to the ceremony, so I don't know how you feel about going?"

"Do you want to go then Mum?" Sam asked.

"Well it's been such a long time since I have seen Sylvie, and I've never even met Caroline, her daughter. I suppose it is good of them to think of us when we have not seen them for so long. But there's no way I could face driving all that way on my own."

"Catrin and I will have a talk about it before we need to reply definitely. At the very least I could come with you and drive you down there, even if Catrin stayed here with Emily."

"That would be very thoughtful, Sam. I do not think I would enjoy going to the wedding on my own and the journey would not be much fun, even if I went by train. When I took you down when you were very young, I went on the train then, but I do not think I could cope with that now. It would be so nice to have your company at the wedding, if you could manage it."

* * * * *

Two hours later Sam and his mother walked into the RSPB Warden's office at the Lake reserve. They had finished their hasty supper and then rung Huw to check if it was convenient to call that evening.

The office had been constructed as a glazed, lean-to extension to the stone-built cottage that Huw shared with his sister and rented from the Estate. It was large and comfortably furnished with a settee which could double as a bed for any visiting RSPB personnel, two easy chairs, a large modern pine desk with matching bookcases, and a small bathroom and kitchenette adjoining.

Sam watched as his mother gave Huw Williams a quick peck on the cheek and patted his grey-streaked beard affectionately. He had wondered at one time if the two of them might get together, although as Huw was his father-in-law, he was not too sure how that would work out. Life could get too claustrophobic, he thought. He had no worries now though, as although they did seem to be quite close, he had never seen any sign recently that there was anything more between them than friendship.

"Thank you for seeing us Huw, especially at such short notice. I know its horrible remembering that terrible day, but I think it is time that Sam knew everything that happened with Ellie. That is why I rang you so urgently. Things all seem to be coming to a head, somehow, and I think Sam should know the full story.

You saw it happen, perhaps you should be the one to explain what you saw, even if none of us really understand fully why it happened."

Huw handed them both a coffee from the kettle he had just boiled in the kitchenette, and then began his story.

"I had not been warden here for very long – Linda and I had not long moved from Birmingham and Catrin was only four at the time. I wanted to return to my roots as I was born just a few miles down the road, but I met Linda at University and found a job in the Midlands.

"After we married, I stayed on there for a few years, but I was always longing to return here, and Linda had a great love of the countryside. It was Linda who saw the advertisement for the job here as Warden for the RSPB, and I jumped at it, as it was everything I had been hoping for. I looked forward to managing the reserve and keeping an eye on the wildlife around the lake. I never dreamed I would witness something so appalling.

"The fact that Catrin was so young, a similar age to Tristan, made it even more dreadful. I was always terrified something would happen to my daughter when she was small and after Linda died, I worried even more.

"The day it happened, I had been watching for a peregrine falcon I had spotted some days before, and had my binoculars ready in my hand when I caught a movement on the opposite shore of the lake. There is a clearing in the forestry, near the road that borders the lake, and it creates a small bay area almost like a tiny beach. There are picnic tables set up on the grassy part and they run the hire boats from there in the summer season. I saw Ellie's turquoise car parked over there near the beach, and a woman moving about by it. I did not know her very well, but I had seen her about, and she used to drive around the lake quite often. The car was very distinctive – not one you could confuse very easily. I think when the lad was small, she would drive him around to help him go to sleep if he were fretful.

"I took a closer look with the binoculars and sure enough it was Ellie. She always dressed in pastel colours, I remember, and I can still see her clearly even now. She was wearing a pink short-sleeve shirt and pale blue jeans and looked more like a child than a young woman. It was a fine, mild day in mid-September, and I watched as she appeared to be clearing up the remains of a picnic, and then lifted up a sleeping child and put him in the back of the car. I don't really understand why I kept the binoculars trained on her at the time – there was just something about her movements, somehow, that held my attention."

He paused to take a mouthful of coffee and then continued,

"I could not quite believe what happened next. In fact, I am still not sure if she really meant to do it, or if it was an accident.... She got into the car and must have released the handbrake. The slope of the beach was just enough to set the car rolling slowly, so slowly it felt like an age, until it tipped into the lake and disappeared. I kept thinking she will stop it, she will put it into reverse, it will be okay .... but it wasn't."

Sam choked on his coffee in shock.

"You mean, you think she did it deliberately, she killed herself and little Tristan?"

"Well it seems unbelievable that she could have done such a thing, but they found traces of sleeping tablets in both Ellie and Tristan. One theory was that she had drugged Tristan until he was unconscious and then taken the same thing herself, getting into the car as soon as she felt sleepy.

"I jumped into the Land Rover, and drove round to the beach straight away, using the walkie-talkie to summon help, but by the time we got there it was too late and there was no sign of the car. When it was finally dragged from the lake the next day there was no doubt of the outcome, as two bodies were still strapped inside."

Sam was still in shock. Why had they kept all the details from him for so long? He could understand it when he was little but surely once he was an adult? But by then he supposed they were trying to put it out of their minds, trying to hide away from the tragedy, pretending it had never happened at all.

CHAPTER EIGHT

It was pitch dark when Maggie and Sam returned to the Mill. Catrin was standing in the doorway, having heard the car pull into the driveway.

"What did Dad have to tell you then Sam?"

"The whole story of what happened with Ellie and the little boy. He actually witnessed what happened."

Catrin was quiet for a moment. She had heard the story before but not in any detail. She had been so young when it all happened, somehow it did not seem real. She listened as Sam repeated what her father had told him. It was all dreadful, she felt, and she would never understand how a mother could do such a thing to her own child. But now something closer to home was troubling her.

"Where's Emily?" Sam asked suddenly, worried by the look on Catrin's face.

"She's having a sleepover with Hari next door. His mum suggested it a while ago and I thought that tonight might be a good time. I wanted to take her mind off…" Catrin's voice trailed away as if she was uncertain quite what to say.

"Off what?" Sam was worried.

"This imaginary friend she has – Trissi she calls him. She said something that scared me today. She said Trissi had told her we must look under the floor in the blue bedroom. Honestly, Sam, it really gives me the creeps when she says things like this."

Sam began to have goosebumps creeping up his spine. The conversation with Huw was still fresh in his mind.

"Mum, what was my cousin's name? The cousin that died with Aunt Ellie?"

Maggie's face echoed the shock in Sam's.

"His name was Tristan," she whispered, hardly believing what she had heard.

Sam shook his head in confusion, "In that case, perhaps we should look under the floorboards straight away – it may all be nothing after all, just Emily's wild imagination."

Sam led the women up to the blue bedroom in the part of the Mill that had been renovated when Maggie and Ellie first moved up from Essex. Although Catrin and Sam had moved into this part of the building, the blue bedroom had remained untouched. A memorial somehow to Ellie, a place that no-one else felt comfortable using, with some of her clothes still hanging uselessly in the old pine wardrobe.

At first, they could see no sign of anything strange. The bedroom had been one of the first to be renovated so that Ellie and Steve could use it. The floorboards had been stripped back and painted a pale blue, and a large antique blue and cream rug covered most of the floor area. They pulled back the rug but could still see nothing.

"Is the bed still in the same place it was then?" Catrin asked Maggie.

"Yes, more or less, I suppose."

They pulled the double bed away from the wall and pushed it towards the door. Underneath, it was immediately obvious that one of the floorboards was loose. Sam put in a hand and felt underneath, bringing up a metal cashbox.

"Is it locked?" Catrin asked.

"No," Sam pushed open the lid and revealed a leather-bound notebook. On the first page was written the name "Ellie" in large letters, decorated almost like an illuminated manuscript with flowers and stars in multi-coloured ink. He flicked through it quickly.

"It seems like some kind of journal,"

Catrin looked at Maggie.

"I think you should take it and look through it, Maggie. You are the only one of us who understood part of what was going on. You should be the one to read it."

"I think I will look at it in the morning," Maggie took it almost reluctantly. "I have been having enough bad dreams lately – this will have to wait until daylight now."

* * * * *

"Have you read it yet?" Sam asked his mother the next morning. She had joined them as Catrin was clearing breakfast away.

"Some of it, Sam. It is very painful, even after all these years. She says no-one was listening to her, no-one had time for her. She had apparently been seeing a counsellor. I don't know how things turned out but obviously it did not help. Apparently, the last straw was when Steve planned to go off on another tour on the Continent. She could not bear to be alone, she said, and she was dreading the winter. I remember she always said she hated it here in wintertime, but I would try to jolly her out of it by talking of plans for Christmas and family get-togethers.

"But she wasn't alone. You and Dad were living in the same complex with her."

"She felt alone Sam. She felt no-one really cared and then something seemed to have happened that was the last straw. Something someone had told her, but she doesn't say what it was."

Catrin was confused and upset.

"How could she do it? I can understand her feeling everything was too much to cope with but why take Tristan with her? How could a mother do that to her child, it just seems beyond cruel to me?"

"I think she genuinely felt it would be safer for him. She talks about all the dangers of the world. I think she felt that if she were not around to take care of him, he would suffer terribly. She had gone to a very dark place and the world looked very bleak to her."

Catrin still found it hard to accept that any mother could do such a thing. How could she even think of leaving the child motherless, let alone take him with her? Catrin had known depression herself, often feeling angry that her own mother had died when she was so young, but she still could not conceive what had been in Ellie's mind.

Catrin had found her mother's death from illness extremely hard to bear. From what her dad had told her, Linda had obviously suffered a great deal before the end, but she was determined to survive as long as possible for Catrin's sake. There had been times in Catrin's own life when she had felt life was not worth living, especially when she had had her heart broken by a boy at Teacher Training College, but she had always been too concerned with the feelings of those around her to seriously contemplate taking her own life. She could not conceive of a situation arising now in which she would want to kill herself and take Emily with her. Rather she would have wanted to carry on living no matter what the cost, to protect Emily and keep her safe.

Her mother had died when she was nine years old, but Linda had always encouraged Huw to speak Welsh with their daughter, and so it was that even though her mother was English, Catrin always felt the culture she belonged to was Welsh. She sometimes felt anger against her mother, and against fate, for leaving her alone, although she knew her mother's death from cancer was inevitable, and Dad had told her when she was old enough to understand that it was a mercy when it came. Dad and Aunt Delyth had done their best to give her a secure and loving home, but even now she still missed her mother. Especially after Emily had been born. She so wished Emily could have known her maternal grandmother and would have loved Linda to have helped her when Emily was a baby.

Aunt Delyth had done her best, but she had never had children herself, and Catrin had so wanted to be able to ask her mother for advice. Aunt Delyth was still very much in her life – sometimes she and Emily would go there for tea after she finished teaching on Friday afternoons. Her Dad, Huw, was often out on his rounds at the reserve but he usually came in for an hour or so before they left.

Maybe because Delyth had no children of her own, she was interested in compiling a family tree, and especially in following the female line, which was a lot trickier.

"Once I've gone there will be no-one to remember the grandparents and the great-grandparents," she would say. She was currently in the process of scouring the local churchyards and parish records for family connections.

"It's no good relying on the men," she had told Catrin. "They just don't seem to have the interest, although I dare say once I have done all the work, they will want to see it!"

Later that Saturday, after hearing Maggie's thoughts on the journal, Catrin decided she needed some space from the Mill. Somehow all the emotions connected with Ellie and the events of that time when she and Sam had only been very young children were getting to her, and she felt extremely on edge.

She walked across to see Sam, now at work in the office.

"I'm popping over to see Aunt Delyth for a while. I will collect Emily from Hari's and we will probably stay for tea. See you a bit later."

＊ ＊ ＊ ＊ ＊ ＊

"Look what I've found now," Delyth was delighted to show off her new discoveries in her genealogy search. Catrin's head was still full of what had been happening at the Mill, but she tried to take an interest in Delyth's revelations.

"I've done well with tracing some of our relatives," she confided to Catrin, "but I've hit a blank with one of my great, great grandfather's sisters – her name was

Sarah and I've found a birth and christening record for her but no burial record. I have even been for a hunt in the local churchyards but there is nothing anywhere."

Catrin found it hard to show enthusiasm for a relative this far back but pretended to show interest for Aunt Delyth's sake.

"I suppose in those days an awful lot of the children died when they were young."

"Yes, the mortality rate in children then was extremely high. And what makes things more confusing, very often if there was a child named, say, David who died, they would then have another son and call that one David too. But somehow, I do not think this one died young. I found some old letters and one refers to someone called Sarah who had just found work at The Plas, the local landowner's residence at the time. Of course, these people often stayed in London for much of the year and it may be she went away to London with them and stayed down there – she may even have married and lived the rest of her life there, but I would love to know what actually happened."

Catrin was glad there would be a family record on her father's side and supposed that one day she would want to trace her mother's family so that Emily had an idea of her roots on both sides. This would be more difficult as her mother was from Birmingham and her Dad had lost contact with Linda's family after she died. There had been a bit of a falling out, she seemed to remember, because they had not come up for the funeral or even to see Linda in her last months. Still at least thanks to Delyth, Emily would know who her relatives were on the Welsh side of the family. Catrin had always felt more Welsh than English, and often found herself thinking in Welsh. She and Sam had decided when Emily was born that they would try to bring her up to be totally bi-lingual, and Maggie had encouraged them.

"It's such a waste not to," she had told them. "If the parents speak two different languages it is so much easier to teach the children both languages from birth – it's much more difficult for them to learn a second language when they get older."

Contrary to her normal scepticism about anything paranormal, Catrin sometimes felt that there was something almost 'fey' about Emily. The 'invisible friend' was unsettling, and they needed to investigate it, but there were other things. On more than one occasion Catrin had heard her talking about things she could not possibly have known about. Sometimes she would even talk about 'grandma' although the only grandmother she had was Maggie, who she called 'Nana'. Sam would say it was because she heard the other children talking and wanted to fit in, but somehow Catrin could not accept that. Most of the other local children called their grandmothers 'Nain' or 'Nana' or 'Nanny'. She had never heard any of the young ones at school or nursery talking about 'Grandma'. She sometimes wondered if the child were referring to Linda, her own mother.

CHAPTER NINE

"Are you sure this is a good idea, Sam? Dabbling with the paranormal frightens me. It could make things worse."

"Amy Rae is booked for tomorrow, Mum. I can't cancel now and anyway I want to find out what is happening with little Emily – we can't just ignore it and she is too young to ...."

The voices die away as they move to another part of the building.

I do not understand what they are saying. Sometimes I hear them talking – the new people – but things are so different now. It is as if they talk a language I have no knowledge of.

Perhaps the boy will help me. It was the boy who woke me from my long sleep. Before he came there was just darkness and silence, with occasional flashes of part-memories, but mainly just confusion. There is so much I do not understand.

Things have been better since the boy came. He said he had come to help me move on. I do not know what that means. He told me he knew about me before – he knew I was here all the time, even though I cannot remember being aware of him when he was still on the other side with the new people.

I know I have been here a long time. The boy says he has been here many years but since he arrived the time passes more easily, and I am sure I was here many, many years before he came. I feel I have always been here, frightened, and lonely in the darkness, but I feel less lonely now he is with me. I do not feel so afraid now. But he is so young, the boy. Sometimes he does not understand any more than I do.

There is a little girl here now – on the other side. She talks with the boy but I do not think she knows about me.

I can see her, but I cannot talk to her.

I feel better since the boy came but I know there is so much that does not feel right. I do not understand why I seem to be trapped here. I am sure this is not where I really belong, but I do not know where I should be either. I wish all this would end. I wish I could just go to sleep again and never wake up.

The boy tells me he is trying to make things better. He thinks the little girl may be able to help us, but I cannot see how she can.

* * * * *

Light from the setting sun, glinting through the budding new growth on the trees, lifted Amy's mood as she left the outskirts of Shrewsbury and headed towards mid Wales. The lanes were dotted with cherry blossom and the white froth of blackthorn flowers, and as she neared her destination, she could even glimpse colourful flashes of wildflowers along the banks.

She had decided to book a two-night stay in the village, although Sam Johnson had offered her accommodation at the Mill itself. She could have managed the daily commute to Shrewsbury quite easily but felt she would be more in tune with the area if she stayed and soaked up the local atmosphere.

It was growing dusk when Amy turned into the village and started to look for the B&B she had booked into. Suddenly she saw it by the bridge and felt relieved. It was a two-storey building which looked quite modern and cheerful, white rendered on the outside with fresh yellow paintwork and baskets of primroses by the door. She guessed it had probably been built in the fifties, long enough ago to have known some disturbances which may have left imprints, but hopefully not too many.

Amy had not wanted to stay anywhere too old. Older buildings had too many shadows and fragments of consciousness all vying for her attention. She had learnt over the years how to screen out the background voices and scraps of sentience that were present in all places of human occupation, but newer properties were usually less exhausting. If she was going to be working in the day, she wanted to be sure of an undisturbed night's sleep at least.

The B&B was situated right on the road with no parking available outside, so she drove up to the car park in the centre of the village. She grabbed her Cath Kidston printed holdall from the back seat, locked the car and started to stroll back towards the B&B, glad of a chance to have a good look at her surroundings.

The village was an interesting mixture. There was a pub that had obviously been a coaching inn in the past, probably a stop off before the difficult journey over the mountain to Bala. From the outside it still retained the look of a black and white Tudor timber-framed building but how much was truly original was difficult to tell. Several of the cottages on the main street had been renovated beyond recognition, but there were still some that retained their roots, giving the village a cosy, traditional feel. Others had been prettified and were obviously second homes, owned by people from the Midlands and beyond, and in the surrounding fields she could see several large caravan sites which must be catering to visitors from Birmingham and surrounding areas.

She felt intuitively that several of the original cottages still belonged to real locals, or at least people who had been local for several generations. She knew, from enquiries she had made previously, that over the past two hundred years or so the land below the mountains had been mined and quarried, and many people had moved into the area both from England and from South Wales. She could feel the history of the area hanging in the air like sparkling dust motes in sunshine.

There had been a time when the village was thronged with a rich mix of people from all walks of life and some of their descendants still lived in the very houses their great-grandparents had occupied in the days before the mines and the quarry closed. There were still signs of the track where the railway had previously run through the village, taking the slate and mineral ore across the border to be processed or sold on across the border. The railway line itself had long since been ripped up and the sleepers put to other uses in the local farms and gardens.

She walked the 200 yards or so to the B&B with care. The road had been widened where possible over the years, but due to the nature of the bridge over the river, there were some places where there was no proper pavement and she was actually walking on the road itself. There was a steady stream of cars coming over the bridge, headlights distracting her in the gathering dusk. She felt they must be commuters coming home from work. Most people would need to travel to Shrewsbury or Wrexham, or even beyond to Birmingham or Chester, to find work, she realised. Apart from farming or tourism, local jobs must be thin on the ground. There was evidence from the shop fronts in the village that there had been several businesses here at one time, but now there was just the one village shop, which seemed to house the post office as well, and even that looked as if it had seen better days.

It took just a few minutes to reach the B&B and she introduced herself to her hostess, a lady in her fifties or so.

"Hello, I'm Amy,"

"Anna Humphreys," the woman held out her hand. She was sensibly dressed in denim trousers, and a tunic that was splashed with blue paint.

"I'm afraid I've been doing a bit of decorating before the season really gets going. I hope the smell of paint is not too much for you. What are your plans for supper – I can make you something a little later if you would like?"

"Some sandwiches or something light would be lovely," Amy said. She never wanted to eat much when she was working. It seemed to get in the way somehow.

Amy followed Anna to her room which had obviously been the first to be renovated, as it was clean and fresh with lemon yellow paint, a small double bed with a palm-leaf printed quilt that matched the curtains, an all-in-one wardrobe/chest of drawers, and a desk with a ladder-back chair. She was glad that Anna was too busy with the painting to stop and talk. She wanted to be on her own to gather all her thoughts for the morning.

She planned to call at the Mill at 10 am the next morning. She always tried to conduct her 'interviews' in as much morning light as she could, she found it easier to communicate then, and felt stronger in herself. Evening shadows could confuse and disorientate, and messages could be mistaken, or even feel very threatening after dark.

In the past, before she felt truly in control of her gift, she had had some unpleasant experiences, when she felt there were forces out of her control. On one occasion, when she was trying to give a reading at a charity event, she was suddenly overwhelmed with a feeling of pitch darkness and pure evil. Amy had looked at the woman in front of her with total confusion. She appeared to be a very ordinary, middle-aged lady who had probably led a rather boring life. To be confronted with this dreadful feeling threw her completely. She was unsure whether the evil came from the woman herself or someone close to her, but she felt unprepared to try to find out. She began to feel faint, and making ill-health her excuse, made her get-away as soon as she possibly could. Even so, she had still had nightmares after the experience. It had taken some time for her to regain the confidence to use her gift again.

Matthew had helped her through this bad time and given her the strength to carry on.

Now she always tried to arrange things so that everything was in her favour, with no advantages to anything on the other side which might have malevolent intentions. Even so, she was anxious. She never knew what exactly she was walking into, and whether she would be able to handle it. It was possible that any intervention on her part could make things at the Mill worse, not better, and in fact sometimes she felt it was as though things *had* to get worse before they got better.

Sometimes she felt like a relationship counsellor, although she was trying to help presences on the other side. In the same way that no-one could really know what was going on in a marriage, so it was that she never quite knew what was going on in any given situation until she was right in the middle of it all.

An hour or so later Anna knocked on the door with a tray.

"I've brought some food to your room if that is okay?"

"Perfect," said Amy, grateful that she would not need to be sociable whilst eating her mushroom omelette.

Later she put her laptop onto the desk and went through the brief notes she had made after Sam's telephone call, and the email he had sent as a follow up. She felt that the 'invisible friend' was just the tip of the iceberg and there were other troubling forces around, which perhaps some of the family could sense without really recognising what was happening. A lot of children had 'invisible friends' but their parents did not usually call in psychic consultants unless there were other factors at work as well.

She finished checking over her notes and made a hot drink from the tray Anna had put in her room. She was delighted to see a selection of herbal teas as well as the normal tea and coffee and poured hot water from the electric kettle onto a lavender blend. As she sat sipping the infusion, she was strongly aware of Matthew's presence.

"Are you worried about tomorrow?" he was asking her.

"Yes, I am always anxious about something like this. It is too important to mess up. When I just give quick readings for charity, people see it as a bit of fun, and I try to keep everything as light as I possibly can. But this is different. This could matter very much to the people concerned, and especially to the little girl."

"You'll be fine," he reassured her. "You are far too sensitive to do damage in any way."

"I hope so, I really do."

PART TWO 1994

CHAPTER TEN

The station car park is reasonably empty as Ellie pulls up by the entrance. She gets out of the Audi to help Maggie and five-year-old Sam with their luggage and waits to wave them off as they head through the entrance.

Maggie has been anxious about leaving her sister as she seems to be heading into another depression, but at least Steve is back from touring now. She also hopes that by involving Ellie in her journey it may give her something else to think about.

She feels that the trip is an important one. She has been trying to get Paul to come down to London with her for years, but he flatly refuses, and she is not brave enough to undertake that long a journey by car. Sylvie and her husband Tom have been asking her to visit ever since they first moved from Chingford, and she thinks it is time now that she did. She knows she could do with a break, apart from anything else. Paul has been especially difficult of late and she needs some space, some time away to think things over.

She has tried to persuade Ellie to come as well:

"A change of scene might make you feel a lot better, and it would be nice for Tristan to see another part of the world, he has not been out of the valley since he was born."

But Ellie is determined she must protect him.

"He is too young yet. I don't think I could cope with all the travelling with him, and there is so much danger out there – accidents around every corner."

Maggie is sad that her sister will not join her for the trip, but at least Ellie has promised to take her to the station and collect her in three days' time when she returns.

Sylvie has asked her to stay longer, but she does not want to be away from Ellie too long, just in case. Memories of her sister's overdose several years before are still fresh in her mind and she is afraid of what might happen if she is away too long.

She has researched the travel well beforehand as it will not be easy to travel with Sam on her own and has found a direct train from Shrewsbury to Euston. After that she plans to get a taxi to Fenchurch Street and then another train out to Sylvie's home in Upminster. She cannot face the thought of dragging Sam through the tube network and feels the underground might frighten him. She remembers as a small child standing on a platform and hiding her face against the curved wall of the station in fright. The rush of hot air as the train clattered in made her think it was a dragon roaring in from the tunnel.

During the ten minutes before the train is due, Maggie buys some snacks and cold drinks, a magazine to pass the time for her, and a Thomas the Tank activity book to keep Sam amused on the train. He is excited about the trip, but she knows that excitement can soon lead to boredom if the journey is too long.

The train is empty when it arrives as it is the start of its journey, and Maggie ushers Sam through the door. He is wearing a small backpack which contains some of his clothes and some reading books, and she takes this from him and puts it in the rack above their seat. Her own bag on wheels she manages to fit into the gap between the seats, so that it is handy when they leave the train.

They settle down and once the train is under way and Sam's excitement has died down, he starts colouring in his activity book. Maggie sits for a while, glancing at her magazine but drifting off into a reverie as the train lulls her into a more relaxed frame of mind. At least they have started their journey safely, and she wants to rest for a couple of hours before coping with the remainder of their travel.

"Is this seat taken?"

Maggie is roused from her reverie as a dark-haired woman of about her own age, wearing a red jacket, stands opposite her.

"No, its fine – please sit down." She smiles at the woman who appears to be rather flustered. Maybe she has had to run for the train, Maggie guesses.

The woman sits down nervously, clutching her large black handbag to her chest as if it is a lifeline, and Maggie is surprised at her continuing discomfort. Sam has given up on his colouring now and has let the regular movement of the train lull him to sleep.

"Is everything all right?" she asks the woman.

"Yes ... well, no, not really." Tears start to well up in her worried green eyes and she looks frightened.

"Whatever has happened?" Maggie is genuinely anxious about her.

"We've been on a family trip," the woman begins,

"Me, my husband and our two children. We were renting this cottage about six miles from the station where I boarded the train. We had been there for three days, but the weather had been miserable, and the kids were getting restless. It was only a small place and we were all getting on each other's nerves, I guess. Anyway, I had a blazing row with my husband, because he expected me to keep the kids under control all the time and did not want to help with anything. We do have rows every so often, but they usually blow over quite quickly, and I think it helps to let off steam sometimes. I decided to storm out of the house in a huff. Usually he calms down then and comes after me, or sends the kids to bring me back, but this time I had only been walking for a little way when a car pulled up. It was the people we had rented the cottage from and they were on their way into town.

"They offered me a lift, and I did not like to say no and tell them what had happened, so before I knew it, they had dropped me at the station. I had grabbed my handbag before I left so I was able to buy a ticket but then the train arrived before I really had a chance to think, and here I am on my way home and I did not really mean it to come to this. I don't know how my husband and kids will cope without me and somehow a row which should have been over in a couple of hours seems to have turned into a big deal, which I never intended." She stops to wipe her eyes and blow her nose, as if ashamed of the show of emotion.

Maggie is silent for a while, not sure what she should say, then asks what she feels to be a safe question:

"How old are the children?"

"Samantha is nine and Nigel is ten."

"Well, your husband shouldn't have too much trouble looking after them – it's not as if they are tiny."

The woman smiles briefly through her tears,

"He has never had a lot to do with them, to be honest. I pushed him into us having this break together because he is normally working all hours. I think that is why we had the row – we are not used to all being cooped up together. But they will probably all be panicking now because they won't have a clue where I am."

"Have you ever gone off before?"

"Yes, but only for a cooling off period. I am usually back within half an hour or so. I would have rung the cottage from the station, but the train came in straight away – they might have the police out looking for me and everything."

"I doubt the police will be interested if you have only been missing for an hour or so. I am sure if you phone once you get off the train that will be fine. It might stop them all taking you for granted if they get really worried."

"I suppose so," the woman wipes away her tears and sits more upright in her seat. She is beginning to take control of the situation now, rather than letting the circumstances run away with her.

"It may be," Maggie hesitantly tries an intervention, "that this is a blessing in disguise. Maybe you needed to make a point that they would all listen to – it might not be the dreadful development you are dreading."

"But John will be so angry with me. He is always in a temper these days – I have to be careful with every word I say."

Maggie is silent, thinking of the comparison with her own life. She is in exactly that situation with Paul, although as Sam is still so young, she feels she has little choice over what she can do. This three-day break was perhaps the first sign of her taking back control of her own life. He did not want to come with her, but she had the strength to decide that she was coming on her own, whether he liked it or not.

The train is drawing into another station now and the woman rises from her seat.

"This is my stop – I won't ring from the station; I will wait until I get home properly. I expect they will all come home now, but that will be up to them. I've proved I can do something without them, but it will be up to John to see if he can manage without me."

Maybe the balance of power has changed, Maggie thinks to herself. Perhaps fate, in the form of the property owner's car, stepped in for a reason.

The rest of the journey to Euston passes uneventfully but Maggie continues to think about parallels between the woman's situation (she has never asked her name, she realises) and her own. Now, Sam is her top priority, and will continue to be, although Ellie comes in a close second.

Sam is incredibly good as they queue for a taxi to take them to Fenchurch Street and from there board the local train to Upminster.

She feels she is extremely lucky to have such a good-tempered child, so many would be fretful and complaining on such a long journey.

Sylvie is there in her car to meet the train. Her house is just a mile from the station, in a leafy street close to the surrounding fields.

"You needn't have come to meet us Sylvie, we could have walked – it's not that far."

"Maybe not for you but what about Sam's little legs? In any case, it's not the easiest street to find if you have never been before."

They pull up outside a detached bungalow a few yards down from a town park.

"This looks lovely Sylvie," Maggie wonders how on earth she has afforded to buy this place in an expensive suburb, and Sylvie must have guessed her unspoken question.

"Oh, Tom and I are only renting. It belongs to a colleague at work and he has let us have it for a very reasonable rent as he is currently living abroad. Tom and I are working all the hours that we can get now, so that we can save up enough for a deposit, and then apply for a mortgage. We would love to carry on living round here, but it might be too expensive.

"It's really convenient because it has such good links to the City on the one hand, and the countryside is just down the road."

Maybe, Maggie thinks, but it is not like *her* countryside. She can clearly hear the constant hum of traffic on the M25 and she misses the clean air of her home.

"When are you and Tom going to come up and stay with us?" Maggie asks as they walk through the paved front garden with its two parking spaces taking up most of the frontage. It has been prettied up with shrubs to the side, and pots full of bedding but still seems rather claustrophobic to Maggie, used as she is to the open spaces of mid-Wales.

"Oh, as soon as I can get some real time off work. I have managed to get a couple of days off for your visit so that I can take you and Sam about a bit, but a longer break might be difficult for a while. You probably will not see much of Tom while you are here as he has had to travel to Birmingham for a few days. I'm not sure whether he will be back before you leave or not."

Neither of them has any idea that Sylvie's trip to Wales will be much sooner than they imagine.

CHAPTER ELEVEN

Ellie is waiting at the barrier when Maggie and Sam return to Shrewsbury. She grabs Maggie's bag as they walk back to the car.

"Where's Tristan?" Maggie asks immediately.

"Oh, he was asleep, so I left him in the car while I waited for you at the barrier."

Maggie is worried, leaving a sleeping child in a Shrewsbury car park, even if only for a few minutes, seems foolhardy to her, but she bites her tongue. Ellie has come to pick them up, after all. She does find it confusing, though. Ellie seems to be so worried about Tristan's safety in some ways, yet she leaves him alone in the car when she goes to meet them. It does not seem to make sense, somehow.

"How was the trip?" Ellie puts Maggie's bag in the boot.

"Oh, great thanks. I enjoyed the break, but I could not go back down there to live. It is just so busy everywhere. Even in Sylvie's street, which is out near the countryside, you can hear the traffic on the M25 all the time, day and night. The skies are always busy too – one night I counted ten different aeroplanes at the same time."

"Yes, it is nice living up here, I suppose," Ellie's approval is qualified. "There are things here that disturb me, though. The farming, for one thing. I hate to think of the animals going off to market. I'm glad we did not think about restarting the smallholding, I couldn't have faced sending animals away to be slaughtered."

Maggie sighs. Her sister has always found it difficult to cope with the hard facts of life. Ellie had hated living in London because it was too noisy and busy, and now she is struggling to handle living in the country.

It is a lovely afternoon in July as they drive back towards mid-Wales. Maggie is delighted to be coming home, even if she did enjoy the change of scenery, and the bustle of London. Nice for a few days, but she would not want to move back down there permanently.

As they leave the outskirts of Shrewsbury, she tells Ellie about their trips up to London. Sylvie had taken some time off from her job at the Stock Exchange to show them around. They had not had a chance to meet up with Tom as he was on a business trip to the Midlands.

On the first day, they had visited the Natural History Museum so that Sam could see the dinosaur exhibition – Sam is currently fascinated by dinosaurs. The second day they had taken a trip on a sight-seeing tour bus, which Maggie and Sylvie felt would be the best way to show Sam a taste of London. They had ended up in a gift shop near Fenchurch Street station where Maggie had bought him a red double-decker London bus as a souvenir, so that he could show it to the other children at school when he got back, and Sylvie had bought him a brightly-coloured plastic dinosaur to keep at home. Sam, true to form, had told her later,

"I'll give the dinosaur to Tristan. He hasn't been able to come with us, but he should have a toy too."

"How was Sylvie, is she well?" Ellie asks, rather coldly.

Maggie remembers that Ellie has never been keen on Sylvie. Perhaps because Maggie and Sylvie were the same age and had often been able to go out together on their own, whereas Ellie was deemed too young to join them. She has always thought there was some jealousy there. Ellie obviously used to feel that Maggie should be at her beck and call all the time.

"Sylvie is fine – she was asking after you and Tristan. I do not know when she and Tom are planning to start a family – now she says they are saving up madly so they can afford to buy a place of their own. The house they live in now is only rented."

"Well, she'll have to get a move on if she wants children," Ellie is dismissive. "Time will be running out soon."

"But she's not thirty yet!" Maggie exclaims.

"The clock is still ticking – they say it is more difficult to conceive the longer you leave it!"

"How are things at home?" Maggie changes the subject. Ellie is being very waspish about Sylvie, and she does not want to encourage this frame of mind.

"Oh fine, I suppose. Steve has been doing a lot of work from the studio while you have been away, but he is planning to go off on tour again shortly, although I have told him I hate it when he is away."

"And how has Paul got on?"

"Well, I haven't seen much of him to be honest. He usually keeps himself to himself when you are not around, and I think he has been doing overtime at work."

Maggie is rather dreading her return to Paul. She will be glad to get home in one way, but she does not know how Paul will react to her act of rebellion in going down to see Sylvie without him.

As they drive into the Mill yard, Maggie is pleased to come home to the building they have so carefully restored. The grey stone is glowing in the summer sunlight and the flower troughs she has lovingly planted under the walls at the front look at their best, filled with apricot begonias, pink petunias, and white trailing bacopa. There is still a long way to go with the outbuildings until their project is properly on track, but at least Steve has his studio to keep him busy. She feels Paul was never really committed to the idea, but he seems happy enough in his commercial library at Chester.

She still feels anxious about seeing him on her return, but hopefully he will have missed her running around after him while she has been away and will be pleased to see her when he gets home from work.

* * * * *

A few days later, Maggie, Ellie and Opal are gathered by the entrance to the old Mill.

"I'll call a taxi," Opal suggests.

"No, no, I'll drive – I can't take much alcohol without feeling ill so it's no sacrifice for me," Maggie insists.

"Okay, but we'll go in my car – I'm insured for any driver, and it will be ...."

"Posher?" Maggie interrupts Ellie, laughing.

"More special, more exciting than in your estate car – that's more like a workhorse."

"True, but it has come in very handy for fetching building supplies and so on."

"That is exactly what I mean, Maggie, hun. It's probably still full of bags of plaster and tins of paint!"

The three women set off excitedly, dressed up in party outfits and looking for some fun. It has been a long time, Maggie realises, since she last wore a sparkly top, or had fun, for that matter. She has found, hanging at the back of her wardrobe, a turquoise, sequinned top that she bought before Sam was born, for a weekend trip to Blackpool. She has paired that with her best black trousers and silver sandals and feels more attractive than she has for years.

It is Opal's idea. A girl's night out to cheer them all up a bit. She had mentioned it when Maggie and Ellie returned from the station two days before. She feels it will be a chance for her to get a bit closer to them. She is very much the outsider at the Mill, and she hopes this evening together will change that.

"The men can babysit for a change. It will do us all good to have some fun. There are several clubs and pubs with music licences in Oswestry, so we won't have to go too far."

Maggie had wondered how Paul would react to the three of them going out on their own for a girls' night, but she need not have worried.

He has been more pleasant since she got back from Upminster. Maybe he has missed her and is trying to allow her a bit more space to be herself. She hopes this will continue but feels he might not be able to keep it up for long. The habit of putting her down and trying to control her has been going on for too long.

A few hours later, Maggie sits at the bar, playing with a glass full of tonic and lime juice. Alcohol always makes her feel a bit sick somehow. She remembers when she had her miscarriage not long after she and Paul got married. She had had to go into hospital for a D & C and had been given a pre-med. She never knew what the pre-med consisted of (just as well perhaps), but it made her feel euphoric, without any accompanying feeling of sickness at all. Like being merry without the discomfort, she had thought. As she was whisked off to theatre, she felt as if she were going to a party. Maybe that is the appeal of recreational drugs, she thinks, although that is a road she can never go down. She has far too much need to be in control of her own actions.

The music is noisy, but the buzz is infectious, and even stone-cold sober, Maggie begins to feel the influence of the excitement, although she is not tempted to join in the dancing. She watches Opal, totally at home and comfortable in this environment, as she gyrates and bops in perfect time to the beat. She looks colourful and exotic in a shiny red jacket and orange trousers and has gathered something of an audience around her. She is oblivious of the attention, lost in her fusion with the music.

The multi-coloured disco lights are flashing in time with the beat, making it difficult to see properly but Maggie eventually sees Ellie towards the edge of the room in her figure-hugging silver mini dress. She looks flushed with excitement and there is a heavy-set man dancing close to her. As she watches he moves in, sweeping her up in his arms and holding her tightly and close. Then he bends over and whispers something. Maggie watches anxiously as they both leave the dance floor and head outside through the open doors at the rear.

Ellie is having a lovely time. The alcohol has given her a real buzz and she feels that she is finally getting the attention she has been missing since Tristan was born. The man she is dancing with is holding her tightly, and she can feel his erection pressing against her. It gives her a feeling of power somehow and she feels swept away with excitement and longing. He takes her out into the car park and presses her up against the wall in the darkest corner.

Suddenly, she does not feel so excited. The fresh air has woken her from her alcoholic haze. The reality of the rough brick wall pressing into her back, his tongue forcing its way into her mouth and his hands roaming all over her body, just seem sordid now, no trace of the romantic excitement she thought she was feeling. She panics and starts to pull away, but he is too strong, and she feels utterly powerless. She hears Maggie shouting for her from the rear door of the club:

"Ellie, are you okay, Ellie?"

The man with her pulls away abruptly and as he does so, she turns her head and is violently sick in the gutter.

"For fuck's sake!". The man, she does not even know his name, turns away in disgust and melts into the surrounding darkness as Maggie comes running up.

Maggie settles Ellie into the car, locking her in, in case the man should reappear, and then turns back to the club to look for Opal. It seems a shame to drag her away when she is obviously having such a great time, but she needs to get Ellie home.

* * * * *

At 10 am the next morning, Maggie goes to call on Ellie.

"How are you feeling today?"

"Oh, much better Maggie, hun. Sorry I was such a pain yesterday – did Opal mind being dragged away so early?"

"No, she was fine – she understood. I think she often disappears off to clubs by herself. It is her world after all, she has been singing on Steve's tours for the last year or so. I think she feels more at home in that environment than she does working in the studio here."

"I worry though Maggie. I think Steve must find Opal much more fun than being with me. I hate the thought of him being away with her, and me not there."

"Well, you and Tristan could go as well. He has offered lots of times."

"Yes, I suppose, but I cannot face taking Tristan with us – something might happen to him. And there is no way I could leave him behind, go without him. I would never have a moment's peace."

CHAPTER TWELVE

The summer storm rages outside, a fury of jagged white lightning tearing the darkness apart. Ellie sits in the bedroom window cradling Tristan in her arms. He had woken, crying with fright at the noise of the thunder, and she had immediately been at his side.

Now as she soothes him and hushes his sobs, she watches the lightning flashes bringing trees and shrubs into sharp definition, framed black against the brilliantly lit sky. Suddenly heavy hailstones, some as large as marbles, beat down on the roof of the building and bounce against the ground, as if the elements are trying to break into the house. The sound is so powerful she fears the storm will destroy the fabric of the building and wash them both away. It has been an awfully long time since she witnessed a storm as intense as this one.

Tristan twists in her arms at the sound of a very loud thunderclap, and Ellie tries to distract him.

"Look how pretty the flashes are, Tristan. They light up the sky like magic fireworks."

"Magic fireworks," he murmurs back, looking interested, "but the noise hurts mummy."

"Yes, it does a bit, honeypie, but the lights are so pretty. See how they make all the trees shine against the darkness."

She remembers that once when she was a child there had been a similar, frightening storm. She and Maggie had both awoken in fright and ran into her their parents' room. Her father was not there, she suddenly realises how strange that was, but her mother pulled them both into bed with her and soothed them, telling them stories until the storm had passed.

On this night, sitting here with Tristan, the storm has given her an adrenaline rush. She feels a rising tide of excitement and exhilaration, the very electricity in the air seeming to energise her and pull her out of the lethargy that has consumed her for so long.

Maybe the energy released by the storm will give her the momentum to retake control, to pull her out of this impasse and help her to start making some decisions. For far too long she has been caught on a hamster-wheel of doubt and worry, overlaid with a heavy blanket of depression. The doctors have given her tablets to help – anti-depressants and sleeping tablets, but she is afraid to take them. If she sleeps too heavily, she will not hear little Tristan when he wakes. When she has tried the anti-depressants, all they seem to do is add to her sense of confusion. It feels as if the hamster wheel is still running inside her but there is a pseudo-happy cloud sitting on the top stopping her from thinking clearly or making any decisions at all.

She remembers her recent visit to the surgery. She was surprised when Dr Andrew offered her sleeping tablets. Her previous overdose and hospital admittance two years before Tristan was born must have been on her record – perhaps Dr Andrew thought she had overcome her suicidal thoughts after the child was born, or maybe he thought, as she is certain Maggie did, that the attempt had not been a serious one, just a cry for help and attention. Sometimes she is not sure herself whether she meant to go through with it. All she can remember of that time is an overwhelming feeling that life had nothing to offer and her future stretched ahead bleak and empty.

After her return from hospital, she remembers, Maggie had tried to be more supportive, taking her for long walks down the lanes, and driving her to the shrine of St Melangell in a nearby valley. They had felt closer than they had been for years. The trips to the little church at Pennant Melangell remain in her memory as a time of peace and comfort. Their visits had only stopped when Maggie became several months pregnant with Sam, she recalls.

"I must ask Maggie to take me there again," she decides, "maybe the tranquillity there will help me. It feels such a spiritual place I may find my answers there." She knows she will not find the energy to make the trip on her own, but with Maggie's help and support it is something she can consider.

Her thoughts return to Dr Andrew. He had also suggested she see a counsellor to talk through her situation, but Ellie is not sure she is comfortable with this. She does not see how talking to anyone can really help her. She has tried confiding in Maggie again, and even attempted to get Steve to take her worries more seriously, but no-one seems to have any time for her these days. They all seem to think that because she has Tristan to take care of, she has less need of their support.

"If only Dad were still alive." She feels sad looking back to the past, "Dad always had time for me, always made a fuss of me. I was always his favourite."

She remembers how it would make Maggie jealous, although her sister would never admit it. Maggie and her mother had been close, but she and her Dad had a special relationship. He used to call her his little princess and that was how he made her feel when she was with him. On Friday nights he would come home from work with presents for both of his daughters, but her present was always the nicest – a new pair of shoes for Maggie, but a pretty dress for her; a pot of crocuses for Maggie, but a miniature rose in a ceramic bowl for her. She remembers the gifts as if it were yesterday. She cannot remember if he ever brought gifts or flowers for their mother. Strange now, thinking back, she suddenly feels that her parents were not close. She cannot remember any signs of affection between the two of them, and Angela had found someone else after she had been widowed. Ellie has never forgiven her mother. After Dad was killed, how could she replace him, how could she find another man to love when Dad had been so perfect?

The storm has subsided now, the hail turning to rain and then the rain settling into a more gentle and persistent rhythm. Tristan is asleep in her arms, and she is beginning to shiver in her thin cotton nightdress. She gently puts him back into bed and returns to her own room. Steve is away, again, and her newly found confidence seems to ebb away with the calming of the storm. Perhaps tomorrow she will find the energy to try to improve her situation. Maybe she will give the counselling a try. Anything to lift this dark lethargy which consumes her very soul.

* * * * *

The next day is clear and bright. The storm has carried away the dust and sultry heat of August and given the landscape a cooler, fresher feel with a promise of autumn to come. Ellie feels re-energised and calls on Maggie after breakfast.

"I thought we might take the boys for a walk to the village – I need to get some milk and it will be nice not to take the car but make an outing of it instead."

Maggie is surprised but pleased. It is good to see Ellie happier and more motivated.

"I'll grab the double buggy – if the boys get tired of walking, we can pop them in. If not, we can use it to carry the shopping." Maggie goes to the Granada and pulls out the pushchair.

They head down the lane towards the village, with both boys excited at a trip that does not involve the car.

"We should do this more often," Maggie says.

"It's just too easy to pop in the car – it is so much quicker," Ellie laughs.

The lane is fringed with long grass, still wet from the previous night, and the boys run ahead and kick at it with their wellies.

In the distance they can hear the drone of tractors. The fields are too wet to harvest after the storm, so they must be occupied on some other task. Looking across the valley they see two tractors climbing the opposite hillside, one green, one red.

Sam loves tractors and shows off his knowledge proudly,

"The green one is a John Deere and the red a Massey Ferguson," he tells Tristan, pointing them out.

Halfway to the village the boys get tired of running about and sink into the pushchair.

"I knew it would come in handy," Maggie laughs.

They reach the village shop and buy milk and bread before turning for home.

"Shall we try the short cut?" asks Ellie.

"Well, if the pushchair can cope with the track."

There is a path that runs roughly parallel with the lane but takes a more direct line. It is impassable in winter as it gets boggy but in the summer months it is dry enough to use easily. The tough reedy grass that fringes the track is evidence of the regular waterlogging.

They turn off the main road and head along the footpath.

"This is where the old railway line to the quarry used to run." Maggie tells Ellie.

"I know. There is not much evidence of it left now, is there – but it is very strange Maggie. Have I told you before? Sometimes when I am in bed at night and everything is quiet, I could swear I hear the whistle of a train."

"That's crazy Ellie. There hasn't been a train along here for 50 years or more, not since the quarry closed."

"I know – but that's exactly what it sounds like."

They make their way back across the field that lies directly below the Mill, crossing the river on the ancient stone bridge which is only strong enough to carry foot traffic.

"You know I've been having some problems, Maggie?" Ellie decides to confide in her sister. "Dr Andrew has arranged for me to have some counselling. I wasn't sure about it at first, but I've decided to give it a try."

"Oh well done!" Maggie gives her a quick hug. "I'm sure it will help and I'm so glad you've agreed to try it."

"There is something else, Maggie hun, if you have time these days?"

"What is that love?"

"Can we go up to Pennant Melangell again sometime soon? I love it there - it is so peaceful. We can tell Tristan and Sam the story of St Melangell shielding the hare from the hunters and being granted the land as a sanctuary. You know ..." she looks at Maggie thoughtfully.

"Yes, Ellie?"

"If ever anything happens to me – I mean if I get ill or something, that's where I want to be buried. Out there in that peaceful place. Sometimes I almost feel it is calling to me in some way."

"Don't be so silly, Ellie. Nothing is going to happen to you. But I do know how you feel about the church there, it does feel very tranquil. We will have to go up there again sometime soon."

* * * * *

Two weeks after the storm Ellie is driving her turquoise Audi, a present Steve had bought her when the band started to earn serious money, to the appointment with Dr Mike Lane, the resident psychotherapist at the Medical Centre. The dusty single-track lane is fringed with frothy white cow parsley and the lush hedgerows hum with the abundance of wildlife. As she slows the car for a bend, she notices a female sparrowhawk shadowing the car, swooping, and dipping above the hedgerows as if to draw her attention.

"How wonderful to have that freedom," she thinks. "To be able to fly away from trouble and carve your own path."

She almost feels that the bird is talking to her, telling her to regain control of her own life, offering her a new beginning.

She books in with the receptionist at the medical centre and is told to wait in the third room on the left. The room is empty when she enters, and she takes the time to have a good look round. Her nerves are beginning to get the better of her now and she needs something else to think about.

The decoration of the room is bland, cream walls, cream paintwork. This must be the default colour for all the consulting rooms, she thinks to herself. The clinical examination couch on one wall must be a standard fitting for all the rooms, but it has been softened with scatter cushions in blue and green hues. There is a soft-focus print on the wall, depicting a lake surrounded by woodland, obviously intended to create a calming atmosphere. A large pine-effect desk fills the opposite wall to the couch, where a computer monitor, and a dictating machine sit. Above the desk are two bookshelves running the length of the wall and filled to bursting with scuffed hard-back books and new paperbacks. A metal filing cabinet sits under the vertical blinds which screen the window. There are two metal chairs, one by the desk and one by the couch, each with an added cushion to soften the effect. The practical vinyl floor is partly covered by a large, Persian-style rug in reds and oranges. She wonders whether these softening touches are provided by the surgery or whether the therapist has chosen them himself.

After a few minutes he opens the door.

"Sorry to keep you waiting," he shuffles some files in his hand and then turns to face her.

"I'm Mike Lane – how are you today?"

Ellie sees a pleasant-looking man about ten years older than herself. His dark-framed glasses give him a professional, reassuring look but his clothes are relaxed, almost to the point of being scruffy, dark denim jeans and a brushed cotton check shirt which needs an iron.

"I'll just make a few notes to start with if you don't mind. We need to keep the record straight."

Ellie is startled. "I want this to be confidential," she begins.

"Oh, don't worry. The notes are only for my own use. It helps to keep track of how our sessions are progressing."

She is finding the appointment disappointing. After taking notes about her age, address, next of kin, he finally gets around to asking how she feels and what is troubling her, but she has already gone through all this with the GPs at the medical centre. She hardly has the energy to explain everything again. Still at least he seems to be listening to her, which is more than her family appear to do. Finally, they get to her dream, the dream that has recurred several times in the last few months.

"I am in the car with my husband and little boy," she tells him. "We are going to see my cousin in London and the road runs between two reservoirs, one on each side. Suddenly, Steve deliberately steers the car off the road and into the reservoir on the right. The car starts to sink, and I wonder how to rescue my little boy ... and then I wake up panicking."

Mike, he has told her to call him Mike, not Dr Lane, looks interested. More interested that he did at first, when she felt she was just another patient, just another box to be ticked.

"So, this recurring dream ... what do you think it is telling you?"

She considers for a moment. "I think it is telling me I have to get Tristan away from Steve, and that Steve will bring us to harm in some way."

"Perhaps we should end there," Mike rapidly makes some notes on an A4 notepad. "I'll see you again in two weeks but in the meantime, I want you to think about the meaning of the dream, and what action you can take, if any, to improve the situation you find yourself in."

As she leaves, he flashes her a quick grin and puts his hand on her shoulder guiding her out of his office. Suddenly she feels there is a connection between them. Finally, here is someone who seems to care.

CHAPTER THIRTEEN

"I know you don't like it love, but it's not as if you are all alone here with Tristan. Maggie and Paul are just next door if you need anything." Steve puts his hand on Ellie's shoulder, but she shrugs it off.

He just does not get it. He has only just returned from one trip abroad but now he is planning another one. She longs to tell him that she needs *him*, not something Maggie and Paul can give her.

"Look, love," he continues, "we had a good trip, not many gigs but we are getting well known in Europe now as a support act for some of the headliner bands. If I can make a bit of money now, we can get on with the project here. Once that takes off, I won't need to go away with the band."

No, but you will probably still want to; she knows him too well. She does not believe that the Dark Skies project will be enough for him even if it does get busy. He will always miss the music and the fans. It has been too much of his life so far for him to just give it all up and settle for a quiet life with her and Tristan.

She remembers the early days of their courtship when he would take her everywhere with him – could not bear to be away from her for even half a day. She had loved being the centre of his world. Over the years she had felt herself slipping further and further down his list of priorities. Now she feels that she and Tristan are just burdens to him.

She tells herself to be strong and proud, not to beg, which would only irritate him further and harden his heart against her. She will carry on with the counselling. Then something else strikes her – perhaps Mike is the future.

She thinks back to their initial session. She felt at the time that she had aroused his curiosity – surely it was more than just professional interest? She convinces herself that there is a connection between them, and she is comforted by the thought that he is attracted to her.

He is good-looking too, she realises. His dark intensity is completely different from Steve's blond wavy locks and guileless blue-grey eyes. He is more like Paul, she thinks. Their colouring is similar, but Mike's looks are less edgy than Paul's, more sympathetic and approachable. She has always felt a bit frightened of Paul – he seems to look right through her sometimes, and he can be very unpleasant to Maggie. For the first time Ellie finds herself wondering why Maggie puts up with the way he treats her. Who knows what goes on in a marriage, she wonders? Even the two people in it often do not have a clue.

She consoles herself after her conversation with Steve by looking forward to her next appointment with Mike. Suddenly she feels more optimistic than she has felt for a long time.

In the meantime, she and Maggie take the promised trip up to Pennant Melangell with the two little boys. The little church lies in deep countryside, sheltered by a ring of hills. They wait for a while, drinking in the tranquil atmosphere that surrounds the churchyard, and then enter to look at the shrine.

"It's funny, hun," Ellie tells her sister, "I've never been one for going to church – well, except for weddings and funerals and that kind of thing, but you know I just love the feeling here. It feels so quiet and so spiritual, as if you can just leave all your cares and worries behind you and rest in this calm space."

"I know what you mean, love," Maggie agrees, "it really does feel like a place of sanctuary. I have often thought it must be nice to go on a retreat somewhere. A rest from all the cares and worries of everyday life. Sometimes I get so tired, I just would like to go somewhere like that for a complete rest from the madness of the modern world."

Ellie looks at her sister in astonishment.

"I never knew you felt like that, Maggie. You always seem so organised, so capable, so in charge of everything."

"Maybe so," Maggie admitted, "but looking after everything does get really exhausting!"

She laughed, trying to make a joke of it, but there were times when the burden of looking after everyone else seemed too heavy for her shoulders to bear.

The boys have been behaving well in the small church but are now beginning to get bored. Maggie has found a little booklet telling the story of St Melangell which she reads out to them.

"It says here that Melangell was an Irish princess who came to live in Pennant as a hermit, escaping an unwanted marriage, and she rescued a hare from Brochwel, Prince of Powys, who was out hunting. The hare took refuge under Melangell's cloak. His dogs fled and the Prince was so moved by Melangell's courage and sanctity that he gave her the valley as a place of sanctuary, and she became Abbess of a small religious community."

The boys enjoy the story. Sam, especially, loves his animals and seems to want Tristan to share in his enthusiasm.

"What is a hare, mum?" he asks his mother.

"Well they are just like big rabbits, really, Sam. Sometimes in the evenings you can see them running in the fields – we will have a look for them next time we are out for a walk after tea."

Tristan is getting restless now, so they reluctantly bring the visit to an end and walk back to Ellie's car through the peaceful and serene churchyard.

As they drive the few miles back to the Mill both children fall asleep in their car seats in the back. Ellie checks them both in the mirror and then feels free to confide a little more in Maggie.

"You know Maggie, hun, I love where we live in the summertime, but I dread the winters here."

"Yes, I think you've mentioned it before, love."

"It's the lack of light, the dreariness." Ellie continues. "Sometimes it feels that there is a darkness lurking in the shadow of the mountains, and in wintertime I can feel that darkness seeping down the valley and into my head somehow."

"But you don't feel like that at the moment, Ellie?"

"No, no. When the sun is shining everything seems fine, but even in summer, when its wet and gloomy, sometimes the darkness seems to be reaching out towards me, to swallow me up."

Maggie looks at her sister with concern. She is beginning to be quite worried about her mental state. At least, she tells herself, Ellie has been trying to seek help at the surgery and with the counsellor. Maggie just hopes that will be enough.

"You know, love, if things get bad you only have to come and talk to me – I'll always be there for you."

"I know, Maggie, but sometimes it feels too much effort to even talk to someone. At least it usually passes when the sun shines." But not always, she adds to herself. Surely Mike will be able to help her through this current phase of depression?

A few days later Ellie is on her way to her second appointment, this time in the afternoon. Today there is no sign of the sparrowhawk, with its promise of freedom, and the day is grey and overcast, saturated with drizzly rain. She does not let this get her down, however, as she is deep into her fantasy about a future with Mike. She is already planning how their relationship will pan out and has written Steve out of the picture completely now. He has obviously lost interest in her and it is time to start captivating someone else.

The interview starts well. He is obviously interested to see her again.

"Have you had that recurring dream again?" he asks, looking at her over the top of his glasses, and running a hand through his dark hair. He looks clever, she thinks to herself, cleverer than Steve, more in tune with her intellectually. She has often felt her mind works much quicker than that of her husband.

"No, but I had a different one. It is similar in a way I suppose. But you will understand better than I do what it is all about.

"We are out walking – I am not alone though I am not sure who I am walking with. There are two other people with me who are well known to me, but I cannot put names to them. We are skirting a river which runs in a large loop and it takes time to find our way around. Whilst we are moving the water rises faster and faster, grey-silver and threatening in the misty day. Suddenly we notice that we are cut off: the ground that we were heading for is disappearing under the swirling torrent. There is one single spur of land left running downhill – do we attempt to cross that? We hesitate for fear of being swept away in the rising flood.

"Suddenly there is no land left, no path to find, the landscape is entirely water, swirling, eddying, powerful and frightening. There is no escape for any of us. And that is when I wake up."

"That's a very interesting dream," he is writing notes on his pad. "What do you think it means?"

"I thought you would tell me," she says, peering up at him from under her lashes.

"But if I tell you what I think it means I may be wrong. It is your subconscious telling you something you need to know. My interpretation might be wrong."

"Perhaps, but I would still like to know what you think."

He considers for a moment.

"I would say that it means you feel circumstances are out of your control, you fear being swept away by events you can do nothing to change. Water in a dream is also a symbol of great emotion, overwhelming emotion in the case of this dream. I will lend you a couple of books about dreams, then you can reach your own conclusions."

He reaches over to the bookcase and pulls out a couple of rather tatty paperbacks.

"I've lent them out a few times before," he is apologetic as he hands them over.

She is a little disappointed. She had thought that she was important to him, he would lend them to her as a special favour, but now it appears this is something he does as a matter of course.

Nevertheless, she takes the books with a good grace and smiles at him playfully. "When shall we meet again?"

"Shall we say another two weeks?"

"Here again, do you mean?"

He looks a little startled.

"Well, yes, of course."

She leaves fairly content with the result of the session. She is sure, more than ever, that there is a connection between them, that she means more to him than just another client, and she feels a rising sense of contentment at the thought. She hopes that tonight her dreams will not be of water but visions of Mike and herself in a more perfect future.

When she returns to the Mill Maggie is giving Sam and Tristan their tea, cutting thin soldiers to have with their boiled eggs.

"How did it go?" Maggie looks up from the work surface.

"Oh, quite well, really," but she is distracted, having suddenly noticed something.

"Do you know Maggie, I haven't really seen it before, but Sam and Tristan are so alike, they might almost be brothers."

"Well, they are cousins after all," Maggie is dismissive. "They probably get all their genes from you and me, and hardly any from Steve and Paul."

Ellie accepts what she has said, anxious to get back to her daydreams of a new life with Mike.

Later that evening as she puts Tristan to bed, she is surprised to have a visit from Paul. Steve is still working in the converted studio they had made in the old barn.

"Hang on a sec," she calls out, "I'll just settle Tris and I'll be there."

Tristan has been more restless than usual, and it takes her some time to calm him enough for sleep. When she comes back to the lounge, she is surprised to see Paul still waiting there. It must be something important.

"I needed to see you," Paul grabs her arm. "I think there are things you need to know. Steve is planning another tour abroad in a couple of weeks' time and has asked Opal to go with him."

"Are you sure Paul? Surely, he would not go away again so soon. He has not long been back here."

"He never seems to settle down here at all does he? One moment he's pleased to be back and the next he's off again."

"But he says he's trying to get the cash so we can finish off the project and then he won't need to go off again."

"Do you really believe he will settle here? Even when the place is paying for itself, he will want to be off again. He doesn't like to be tied in one place too long – I've noticed it before."

"Maybe you are right but how are Tristan and I going to manage if he is off all the time?"

"That's why I'm here Ellie. I am certain Steve and Opal are planning to be together permanently, not just on the tour. I think he will leave you and Tristan and be with her instead. You know I have always wanted you – from the moment I first met you after I was engaged to Maggie. You were already married to Steve then, but I did not think he deserved you. I thought that he would treat you badly and that is what he has done. I know I would look after you properly."

"But, but … you've never mentioned any of this before."

"I was biding my time – and I wanted to be sure of you before I said anything to Maggie."

"But what about Maggie, and Sam? How would Sam manage without his Dad?"

"Ah, but you see Ellie, I am not sure I am his Dad."

"What on earth do you mean Paul?"

"All I can say is that Maggie and Steve were very close when you were in hospital that time …"

Ellie is overwhelmed by shock. Paul's declaration and his suspicions about Sam have stunned her. She remembers her surprise earlier about how alike the two boys were. Perhaps he is right, but how could Maggie… how could Steve…, how could they both betray her when she was at her most vulnerable?

Suddenly she bursts into tears.

"Go away, Paul, go away now. I can't deal with all this, it's too much" she almost pushes him out of the door.

"Remember I am always here for you," he assures her as he leaves.

But it is not you I want; she thinks through her confusion. I used to want Steve, but he was not worth it. Now all I can think about is Mike. Mike will help me to deal with all this.

Before she tries to settle for the night, Ellie makes an entry in her diary.

Paul came to see me. I cannot believe what he said. If it is true it means they have all betrayed me - Steve, Maggie, Opal. Everyone I had relied on for support and this is how they treat me. How can I go on, how can I manage on my own, with Tristan to take care of as well? It is all too much to cope with alone. I can hardly write for tears now – life is so hard, so difficult. Everything is grey and dreary.

I will ring Mike tomorrow. He is my only hope now. He is the only person who really cares what happens to me.

Now she has decided what to do she feels she can finally settle for the night. She takes a sip of the camomile tea she drinks at bedtime. It does not always help but sometimes it can be useful to relax her. As she slips the diary back into its hiding place under the loose floorboards, she hears it as plain as day, a train whistle shrilling hauntingly in the darkness.

"It can't be anything else," she thinks, "I must tell Maggie tomorrow."

After a restless night she rings the surgery first thing.

"Can you give me Mike Lane's phone number please. It's very urgent."

"Sorry, Mrs Reynolds," the receptionist is being very unhelpful, "we are not allowed to give out telephone numbers – I'll ask him to ring you, shall I?"

"Yes please," Ellie almost stamps in frustration, "As soon as possible, please. It is very urgent."

* * * * *

The turquoise car is conspicuous in the layby as Mike Lane pulls up in his Range Rover.

"What is so urgent Ellie? Why couldn't you tell me when I rang? I've had to rearrange several appointments to meet you here."

Ellie is shocked that he should be so bad-tempered. Doesn't he want to help her, to be with her?

"I needed to see you Mike. Things have gone so wrong at home, nobody wants me around, no-one cares about me anymore, only you."

Mike looks worried and sits twisting a heavy gold ring on his finger. She finds it strange that she has never noticed the ring before. Is he married then? Would it matter? Perhaps he is unhappy too.

"I have a professional concern for you Ellie. That is all it is, professional. We need to keep our relationship purely on that level or I will not be able to counsel you any longer. As it is …."

Ellie bursts into tears. She knows he cares about her really. Maybe he just does not realise it yet. She peers up at him, helplessly, through her tears. In the past this has worked on everyone when she does not get what she wants. Even Steve has been known to give way when faced with Ellie's tears.

She underestimates Mike though.

"No, Ellie, I can't help you any longer. You are becoming dependent on me, it is a classic problem with counselling, and I am going to have to refer you back to Dr Andrew. I am sure he will find someone more suitable for you to talk to. An empathetic woman perhaps. I have a colleague, Vera, she might help you. This situation is dangerous for both of us."

Ellie cannot believe what she is hearing. What does he mean, dangerous for both of them? Surely, they are soulmates and meant to be together for ever? Steve was a mistake; she realises that now. Mike is her true soul mate. How can he deny it?

She watches in disbelief as he gets back into the Range Rover and leaves her standing desolate at the roadside.

As she watches his car until it moves out of sight, Tristan starts calling to her fretfully, wanting to be released from the confines of his car seat. She leans into the car to comfort him.

"Never mind, honeypie," she coos at him, "we still have each other."

She calls at the village shop for some sandwiches and drinks – they will have a picnic down by the lake. As she puts her purse back in her bag, she checks for the bottle of sleeping tablets. It is still there.

CHAPTER FOURTEEN

Mike curses himself as he drives away. He knows he handled that meeting very badly. Perhaps if he had not been so worried about Janey, he would have realised that Ellie was becoming fixated on him. He has known it happen before, but not so quickly as this. His mind has not been fully on the job since Janey's initial diagnosis and tomorrow they are due to see the specialist in Birmingham for the results of her tests.

He has already cancelled all his appointments for the next week to give them time to decide what needs to be done.

Mike arrives back at the surgery and writes up his case notes about Ellie so that her next counsellor can have some background on her.

"Any chance of a word with Dr Andrew?" he asks the receptionist.

"He's just finished seeing one patient now – I'll check with him on the intercom."

The consulting room door opens and Laurence Andrew beckons him in.

"Hi Laurie," Mike shakes his hand. "I've hit a bit of a snag with one of my clients. I thought I should let you know the situation as I am off to Birmingham tomorrow and I am not sure how things are going to pan out with Janey. It's about Ellie Reynolds."

He explains what has happened and how it seems Ellie has become romantically infatuated with him.

"I've told her that I can't see her anymore. I might not have been able to anyway, the way things are with Janey, but she did not take it at all well. I have said I will refer her back to you and you might find someone else for her to talk to. I think she really needs someone to bring her back down to earth, perhaps an older, more mature woman might be able to help her. I did think of Vera Spencer if she is available. But I certainly don't think she should have a male counsellor; she is too vulnerable and impressionable now."

"I'll give it some thought Mike. I am not sure if Vera is free, but I will get in touch with her. We will need to find a temporary replacement for you anyway until we know how things go with Janey. Good luck tomorrow, I hope it all works out for you."

"So do I, Laurie, although I can't say I am very hopeful. The tests have been very intensive – they must think there is something nasty going on."

Mike leaves the surgery feeling a little more comfortable. He has done everything he can now to help Ellie, everything short of falling in with her plans for him to be her future.

* * * * *

"I'm worried about Ellie." Maggie leans against the studio door, arms folded protectively around her, as Steve takes off his headphones and looks up from the recording console. Sometimes she still feels a sharp pain in her chest when she looks at him. His grey-blue eyes are so expressive, sometimes warm, and glowing, but on other occasions, like today, they can be cold and distant. He and Opal are practising some material for the next tour, and he obviously does not welcome the interruption.

Maggie continues to express her worry, despite the lack of encouragement. Her concern is very real, and she needs him to take it seriously. In the opposite corner of the room Opal is watching her closely and cannot fail to hear the conversation.

"She went out this morning without a word. She has taken Tristan and the car has gone. Normally she lets me know if she's popping out."

Most of the time leaving Tristan with me, Maggie thinks to herself.

"Well, she has been a bit up and down lately. You know how she is. A bit clingy, too, if she thinks I am going away too much. But she was in bed when I got back yesterday. I just thought she wanted an early night and did not disturb her. If I think she is tired I sleep in the spare room."

"She didn't say anything breakfast time?"

"No-oo," he considers, "she was busy fussing around Tristan when I left to come here."

"I'm sure that she's not herself now, I can tell when she disappears inside herself somehow. I know she's been going to the surgery – I just hope they haven't put her back on the tablets, I think they make things worse."

"You think she might do something stupid, like she did before she had Tristan?" Steve picks up a cheap plastic biro from the top of the console and breaks it between his fingers.

"Well, it's possible. And I don't think either of us have been particularly supportive lately."

"I know, I know. But it gets so tiring trying to prop her up all the time – she can be so demanding; it wears me out. She hates me going away and I did tell her I will be off on tour again soon. I did not want to listen to her going on all the time. I keep out of her way when she starts to do that."

Maggie sighs, "I know, I get impatient too. I want to tell her to count her blessings, not dwell on what she thinks is missing from her life, but she just thinks I am insensitive. Well, I suppose we must just try to jolly her along a bit more and listen to her when she needs to have a moan."

She pauses to think for a moment and then continues:

"I might ring the surgery to see how they think she is. Not that they will tell me much, patient confidentiality and all that, but Dr Andrew might help, perhaps, if he realises how worried we are about her."

She leaves Steve to carry on his practice session with Opal. As she turns to leave the singer smiles at her uncertainly, twisting a braided lock of hair around her fingers. Maggie can tell she feels uncomfortable hearing their worries about Ellie but is reluctant to intrude on their concerns.

'I won't say any more until Steve and I are on our own,' Maggie thinks. She tries to ring the surgery for some information, but the administrative staff are unable to comment on her sister's case. They suggest that she makes an appointment to see Dr Andrew to 'discuss her concerns about her sister'.

This might be a good idea, she thinks, at least she can tell him how worried she is now about Ellie's state of mind, even if the doctor will not tell her anything in return. It would help her, too, to talk things over with someone a little more detached than those closest to her and Ellie.

Dr Andrew is booked up for the rest of the week, but she makes an appointment for the following Wednesday.

* * * * *

At lunchtime there is still no sign of Ellie and Tristan. Maggie grows increasingly anxious as the afternoon wears on. Usually Ellie's trips out with Tristan are short, she finds it difficult to keep him occupied if they are gone for any length of time. Maggie is sure her sister thinks the world of Tristan, but she sometimes seems to lack a natural mothering instinct and starts to feel overwhelmed if she spends too much time alone with him. Maggie feels she often spends more time with her nephew than Ellie does, at least during the daytime.

At teatime, to try to put her mind at rest, Maggie puts Sam in his outdoor shoes and anorak and takes him down to see the scout camp in the bottom field. The September afternoon is disappointingly grey, but the earlier rain has cleared up.

There are six neat tents aligned in a row down by the brook. She likes having the scouts there. They always clear up after themselves and leave the place tidy, not like some of the campers they have had since they opened the site.

The campsite was the first thing they opened once they had tidied the area and even before they started work on renovating the Mill. At least it brought in a trickle of income until they were ready to take the project further.

Sam loves to see the older boys although he is shy and usually hides behind her for a while before talking to them.

There are a dozen or so lads kicking a ball around the field, and the leader calls out to Sam, jokingly.

"Do you want to join in for a game of football?"

Maggie smiles as Sam hangs his head and looks worried.

"I think you are a bit young for that yet," she reassures him, smiling encouragingly at the scout leader who is so obviously trying to be friendly and wants to engage with the little boy.

They stop and watch the play for a while until the wind starts to blow chilly.

"I think it's time to think about making tea", she tells Sam.

As they make their way back up to the Mill yard, Maggie's heart stops as she sees a police car turning into the driveway. Is this what she has been dreading all afternoon?

How bad can it be?

* * * * *

Opal is walking back to the guest room in Maggie and Paul's part of the Mill, when she sees the police car pulling into the yard. She has been staying with them while she and Steve plan their forthcoming trip to Europe. She stands back and waits while two uniformed police, one male, one female, get out of the vehicle and knock at the door. In the meantime, Maggie, and Sam, are approaching from the side of the building. As they near the door the female officer calls out to Maggie.

"Mrs Johnson, can we come in and talk to you? We have some bad news."

Opal retreats to the safety of her own room, her heart beating wildly as she wonders what the news could be.

An hour later, she has been called down to Maggie's living room to hear the terrible news that Ellie and Tristan are feared drowned. Their bodies have yet to be recovered but there is really no hope. Opal cannot take it in at first. She can see that Maggie and Steve are both devastated, and Paul looks angry somehow. Amid all the grief and worry she still finds time to wonder why he should be angry.

She waits a little for the news to sink in, and then follows Maggie out to the kitchen when she goes to make them all a drink.

"Would you rather I went to stay in the village for a while, Maggie? There is so much to think about, would it make it easier?"

"No, no," Maggie tries to smile. "If you are here, we have to try at some kind of normality – otherwise we might just all fall apart. It would be helpful if you could be around while we make some of the arrangements as well."

Practical Maggie, Opal thinks to herself, still trying to organise everything, hold it all together. She envies Maggie's strength of purpose but does not guess at the depths of desperation that underlie the calm exterior.

Early the following morning, well before breakfast, there is a knock on her door. She has had a bad night herself. She cannot take in what has happened, what could have driven Ellie to do such a thing. She grabs a shot-silk damson-coloured wrap to put over her flimsy nightdress and opens the door. Paul is standing there, looking as if his world has imploded. She has never really liked Paul, but he looks so upset she cannot help feeling sorry for him. After all, they are all suffering, and she is the one who had the least emotional connection to Ellie.

"I have to talk to someone," he runs his hands across his face and through his hair.

She is surprised, but then realises that she is the outsider, the safest person to confide in. The least she can do is listen to the others and try to help them deal with the tragedy.

When Paul finally leaves her room, she is shocked to see that he has been there for over an hour. She has promised to tell no-one what he has told her about his conversation with Ellie the night before she drove into the lake.

In the coming days she finds it hard to keep Paul's secret, feeling Maggie at least should know, but she has given her word and feels obliged to stay silent.

During the following week she does what she can to comfort Steve. She has always been fond of him, although she would never have tried to steal him from Ellie. She has had experience of brief affairs with 'spoken for' men, and they never worked out well, always leaving her damaged somehow and with a feeling of low self-worth. She realises suddenly that, apart from a few teenage fumbles, she has had very few relationships with unattached men, always being drawn to the unattainable somehow. Perhaps her history with her father has made her frightened of commitment, especially after her mother's experience.

A week after the tragedy, she goes with Steve to Chester to see his agent and cancel his forthcoming commitments with the band. After leaving the office, at her suggestion, they stop for a tea-time snack in a basement café in The Rows.

The café is popular and busy, and they walk through to the back past the central serving area. They wait a while and then a young waitress arrives to take their order.

"Just two teas and two scones," Opal orders for them, taking charge as she can see Steve is not coping very well at all.

"And what will the little boy have?" the waitress waits with her notepad.

"What little boy?" Opal is confused.

"Oh, I'm sorry. When you came in, I was sure .... I thought I saw a little boy with you."

"What did he look like?" Steve suddenly looks up.

"Well he was about three years old, nicely dressed with light blond hair, and he had a really sweet smile which caught my attention – but I must have been mistaken. He must have been with someone else..." She looks flustered and backs away to get their order.

Steve and Opal look at each other.

"Tristan?" Steve murmurs.

Opal feels shivers down her spine and her whole body turn cold.

Some minutes later an older woman arrives with their order.

"Where is the young girl?" asks Opal, wanting to hear more about the little boy.

"Oh, she wasn't feeling very well. The boss has sent her home. She is extremely sensitive. Just between us

I think she is a bit touched. She keeps 'seeing things'. She says this place is haunted by Roman soldiers – I mean, I ask you! I blame all those ghost-hunting trips for tourists myself – I think it puts ideas in her head." She stalks off, shaking her head.

As they drive home, Steve breaks the silence between them.

"I sometimes think I see him too, Opal," he admits. "It frightens me, I don't know how to deal with it. I just cannot do this Opal. I cannot cope it. I will have to go away. Losing Ellie in such a way would have been bad enough, but she took Tristan as well, how can I live here with that? Why does he come to see me, what does he want me to do? It's just all too much and I don't want to feel he is following me around all the time, I can't bear it!"

* * * * *

In bed that night, Steve cannot believe how everything could have gone so wrong. It is all too much for him to take. He had thought all the signs were so good. They had been on track with the Dark Skies idea, and their customer base was growing fast. They had had a lot of enquiries from campers and youth groups anxious to explore the night sky away from the light pollution of the city. If he had been able to continue touring in Europe for a couple more years, they might have had enough funds to complete the renovation of the old stable block and install the observatory that was their eventual goal.

He does not know when Ellie's mental health became so compromised. He had thought that once Tristan was born, she would be happier and more content, and at first that appeared to be the case. He knows that he could have done more to support her. He should have taken her concerns about his absence more seriously. It just seems so hard that her mental health should have broken down at a time when everything seemed to be going so well. Losing Ellie is bad enough, but losing his little son is so dreadful he does not think he can bear it. He feels he is going out of his mind himself.

He cannot believe what happened in the café. His marriage to Ellie had been wearing him down, her unhappiness like a weight around his neck. He had never believed for one second that she might contemplate killing herself and taking Tristan with her. He was just beginning to come to terms with the tragedy, although the pain would never go away however long he lived. Then to have that girl ... she was imagining things, he tells himself. How could she have described Tristan though? How did she know what had happened? Even if she had just picked up on his heartbreak, why did she say it was a little boy she saw? His head spins as he tries to make sense of what has happened. All of it is unbelievable somehow. None of it can ever make sense no matter how much he tries to rationalise it.

In the end he decides he must just shut it all away – trying to deal with it is just too painful. He retreats inside himself, like an animal in pain hiding away in a hole.

He knows Opal is trying to help but it is no good. No-one can reach him anymore. It will be a long time before he can ever have any kind of relationship again

– the pain of losing Tristan in such a way has torn him apart.

A few days after the café visit, his agent telephones him with a job offer from America. They want him to write and record some of his music for a film soundtrack. He does not feel capable of writing any new material, but the offer is a lifeline, an escape route. He grabs it quickly before it can disappear and leaves for America the following week.

CHAPTER FIFTEEN

Three weeks have passed since that dreadful day when they heard the news about Ellie and Tristan, and Maggie is still trying to make sense of what has happened. She knows she will live with the guilt and grief for the rest of her life. She feels guilt for not realising how desperate her sister was, and really devastated that she had failed to protect Tristan from the consequences of her sister's illness.

The police had taken the view that it was a tragic accident and the coroner had echoed that to spare the family, although both bodies had been found to contain traces of sleeping tablets.

The statement had been made in court that perhaps Ellie's foot had slipped when she was trying to manoeuvre the car and she had pressed the accelerator instead of the brake and sent the car spinning into the lake.

Maggie knows this is not true. She has already spoken with Huw Williams at the lake, and she knows that it was a deliberate act on Ellie's part. She feels it is strange though that Ellie did not leave a note for any of them, did not even want to say goodbye.

Steve has left her to get on with all the funeral arrangements – does not want to know a thing. The post-mortem has delayed the funeral, and he has already left for America before it has happened.

She feels the loss of her mother even more now. Angela had had a fatal heart attack within months of emigrating to Australia and had never had the chance to meet her grandchildren. At least, Maggie feels, she was spared the pain of losing Ellie and Tristan so tragically.

Her major support now is her cousin Sylvie who has come up to stay with her and help with the funeral arrangements. She has taken a few weeks leave from her City job and Maggie is so grateful for her help. Paul has been moody and irritable ever since he heard the news, and she feels she is walking on eggshells every time she has any contact with him. It is such a relief to have someone else to lean on, even just a little.

Sylvie has taken a taxi from the station, to cause the minimum fuss by her arrival and is really impressed when she sees the work they have carried out to the old Mill.

"You've made a really good job of this," she takes off the silk scarf she wears around her neck and waves it in the direction of the main building. She is determined to begin her stay by keeping the conversation away from Ellie as much as possible.

"It's still not finished," Maggie tells her. "We still have some of the outbuildings to renovate. We did have several bookings for the holiday accommodation but after the tragedy we just had to cancel them all. We could not face seeing strangers with all this going on."

Sylvie can resist asking no longer,

"Why, why do you think she did it? Did you realise what a state she was in when you and Sam came down to stay with me?"

"We don't really have any clear idea. We know she was depressed – well, she was always up and down – everything was always terrible one moment, wonderful the next. She told me only a few weeks ago that she had arranged to see a counsellor at the surgery. I thought she was coping with everything. She had not said much lately, but I know she hated it when Steve was away on tour, and she thought he was about to leave again."

"I would have come to visit sooner if I thought it would have helped."

"I don't think it would have made any difference, Sylvie. She was always a bit jealous of you, I think. She envied your success in the City, and before that she seemed to resent our friendship. Especially when we both went down to stay with Grandma and Grandad in Eastbourne that time, and Mum told her she was too young to go with us."

"Have you heard anything further from Steve? I know he must have been devastated by what happened, but I don't know if running away to America would make it any easier to live with."

"I had a letter yesterday, actually. I think he realises he still must come to terms with everything even if he is on the other side of the Atlantic. He does apologise for leaving me to sort everything out. One thing he has done, though. He has put the share of Nant-y-felin that he automatically inherits from Ellie into Sam's name, to be held in trust until Sam is 25, with me as a trustee so that I can access funds if we need them in the meantime."

"Well at least that is something, I suppose. It would have been too hard if he had expected you to pay out Ellie's share to him. I suppose he put it in Sam's name as he is his nephew."

Maggie says nothing about his other possible motive. She has previously told Steve she thinks he is Sam's real father and feels that is the real reason he has put the property into the boy's name.

* * * * *

The funeral is just as difficult as they were dreading. Maggie finds it passes in a haze. She automatically goes through the motions of talking to the other mourners, friends and relatives who have come over just for the one day to show support, and the local people who wish to demonstrate their own grief and loss. Maggie and Ellie have only been living in the area for a few years, but the villagers have always made them feel welcome and taken an interest in their work at the Mill. There have been the occasional jealous mutterings about outsiders coming in to take over, but most people are genuinely pleased to see the derelict Mill building restored and given a viable use once more.

Somehow Maggie and Sylvie get through the day and when the two coffins, one normal size and one tiny, are lowered into the grave in the small churchyard, they hold each other close before throwing the roses that they both carry, red for Ellie, white for Tristan, into the open grave site.

On the following day Maggie and Sylvie return to the graveside. It has been neatly filled in, the loose soil mounded over the top, and floral tributes covering the whole area in a dazzling display of colour, shimmering in the autumn sunshine.

"I'm glad we didn't say 'No flowers'," Maggie tells her cousin. "It's comforting to see that everyone thought so much of Ellie."

"Yes," Sylvie agrees. "Some people think floral tributes are wasteful, but it is good to see how much people cared about those who have passed over."

Maggie's own wreath, a cross of white and yellow roses and chrysanthemums, has been placed at the top of the grave by the undertakers, with Sylvie's traditional wreath of white lilies and red roses just beneath, but there are so many flowers it is hard to see which is which. Amid their grief it is still heartening to see how much the tragedy has affected the whole community.

As they stand by the grave, Maggie suddenly finds it odd that she has chosen a cross. She is not particularly religious. In fact, she stopped going to church many years before, when she found she was too busy disagreeing with what the priest was saying to pay much attention to the rest of the service. Somehow, however, she finds the symbol of the cross comforting and reassuring, though what hope she can take from Ellie's death is hard to fathom, especially when she feels so much personal guilt and responsibility.

The two women stop and gaze at the flowers for several minutes, taking time to appreciate the condolences from so many people outside the immediate family.

"Let's hope they are both at peace now," Maggie sighs.

* * * * *

That night they try to eat some supper, still too full of emotion after the visit to the churchyard. Laura, from the neighbouring farm, has brought them a lamb casserole.

"To keep your strength up because I don't suppose you feel like cooking."

Maggie tries to turn the conversation with Sylvie away from Ellie, although everything they discuss seems to lead back to her.

"It's so sad that family often only get together for weddings and funerals, we should make more effort to meet on other occasions. Mum's funeral was an incredibly sad time. We had only just started work here and when she died so suddenly Richard made all the arrangements and she was buried in Australia. I went over there and stayed for two weeks but Ellie refused to come at all. I wish I had asked her more about my Dad, and about her Welsh connections. All I know was that the man who left the Mill to her was her great uncle and there had been some kind of family rift, so I don't think she knew much about him at all."

Sylvie is Maggie's cousin on her father's side so she cannot help with any information.

"You may be able to trace that side of the family through Ancestry or something similar," Sylvie suggests. "It might also be worth looking through the burial records and so on at the local churchyards."

"Yes, but he was a Roberts apparently, which makes things a lot harder. Roberts is the most prevalent surname in this part of Wales. Do you know much about Dad's side of the family – I know we were only seventeen when he died – did you come to the funeral? I can't remember."

"I'll have to do some research – it will be interesting to find out a bit more about the family. I did come to the funeral, I remember. It is all a bit hazy now, but I recall my mother saying something strange happened.

She and I were standing by the graveside after your mother and most of the other mourners had moved on, when a strange woman came up and threw a flower into the grave. Neither of us had any idea who she was, and she turned away quickly before we could ask her anything."

"Mum never mentioned that," Maggie is surprised.

"I expect she was completely unaware of what had happened. My mother did not want to cause any fuss, so I doubt she told her."

* * * * *

A week before Sylvie is due to go back to London, Maggie suggests a trip to try to lighten the mood a little.

"There's a coach outing from the village to Llandudno tomorrow and there are still a few places free – would you like to go? We could take Sam and give him a break from all the misery here."

"I think that's what we all need, Maggie. A change of scenery will be good for us."

The trip is a private arrangement so the coach travels direct without any further stops, reaching Llandudno in plenty of time for them to explore a little. The day is pleasantly warm for October, with a mild breeze that refreshes without being too cold, and they stand on the promenade, near the palm trees, looking out on the grey-blue sea.

"Have you ever been here before, Sylvie?"

Her cousin shakes her head, as Maggie continues,

"Paul and I came for weekends a couple of times before Sam was born, but we haven't been since. I am not sure why – other things got in the way, I suppose.

Shall we take the tram up to the Great Orme – we have plenty of time before the coach leaves again?"

They walk up the side streets to the tram station and buy tickets up to the top of the Orme. Sam loves the tram; it is something completely different that he has never seen before.

At one point the tram tracks cross a road, and Sam is delighted to see the traffic lights that keep both types of transport apart. Half-way up they have to change over to another tram and take a look at the winding station that moves the trams up and down the Great Orme. Sam is fascinated to see the machinery working as it pulls the trams up the steep incline.

At the top of the Orme there is a complex of gift shops and cafes, all undercover in case the weather is bad, and they buy a snack lunch there before leaving the buildings and walking over to the part of the headland that overlooks the ocean. The wind is fiercer here, but the breath-taking view makes it worthwhile – they can see across the Menai Straits to Anglesey, as well as further headlands to the south. After a while they head back to the shelter of the gift shop.

"You know, something about this place reminds me of Eastbourne," Sylvie recalls.

"Where Grandma and Grandad lived? I suppose it's the Victorian buildings, but that explains why I felt so much at home the first time I came here, I suppose."

"Do you remember when we went down to stay with them when we were 15?"

"Yes, during the school holidays. My dad drove us down on the Saturday and your Dad came to pick us up the following week."

"Poor Grandma struggled with us, though, didn't she? She was not sure about how much freedom we should have. Do you remember we both bought stuff to colour our hair that week?"

"Yes, and she was very suspicious but could not be sure, so she could not really say anything! We both found it very funny at the time, but I suppose we were a bit mean really. It's sad we never had the chance to go down again on our own."

"Yes, we had a couple of family weekends there separately didn't we, after that, but it was the only time you and I were there together on our own."

"Grandma probably told the parents she didn't want the responsibility a second time." Sylvie laughed as she remembered.

"Maybe, but after that we both started having boy-friends and separate social lives, and your family moved further away."

The two women are quiet for a moment, remembering that the tragedy of Maggie's dad's accident a year or so later had changed all their lives completely. The shock of his death had contributed to both of his parents dying within the next few years.

"Mum, mum", Sam is pestering Maggie to buy him something from the gift shop. Finally, they settle on a wildlife book written specifically for young children and a large toy lamb, which he holds tightly under his arm.

"Sam certainly loves his animals," Sylvie ruffles the boy's hair.

"He does indeed, but I think he will be too soft to be a farmer – he would never want to take anything to market!"

"He'll have to find a different occupation then, one where he can look after the wildlife rather than rearing animals for food."

"I suppose so, but it's like I always say, if no-one wanted to eat meat there would be no sheep or cattle in the fields. I did think about becoming vegetarian once," she confides to her cousin, "but then I read something about vegetables feeling pain when you cut them up, and I thought well - its them or me!"

Sylvie laughs. "As long as the animals are kept in kind conditions and treated well – that is the important thing."

* * * * *

While her cousin is still staying with her and available to look after little Sam, Maggie has been making some inquiries of her own. She has been in touch with Huw Williams on several occasions to be sure of his thoughts on seeing Ellie at the lake that day. She also contacts the surgery but is given evasive answers. No-one is prepared to admit that Ellie might have been given inappropriate treatment. When Maggie asks to contact the counsellor, she is told that he has moved away to Birmingham and they do not have a forwarding address. She feels that they have closed ranks against her, and she will not discover any more of the circumstances around Ellie's death in that way.

PART THREE –
2019-2020

CHAPTER SIXTEEN

The sunlight streaming through the thin curtains in her room at the B&B woke Amy. The room was bright and cosy, and the sunny glow echoed her own mood. The doubts of the night before had lifted, and she felt ready for the task before her.

She had asked for breakfast at 8.30 and it was there waiting for her in the small front dining room which overlooked the main road through the village. She had refused the offer of a cooked breakfast the night before, but appreciated the croissants, fruit, and coffee that Anna had put out for her.

As she ate, deciding on her plan of action for the day, Anna put her head round the door.

"Is there anything else I can get for you, dear?"

Amy realised that if her mother had lived, she would have been about Anna's age. As she had that thought a flash of vision crossed her mind – Anna's husband dying from a heart attack just after they had opened the B&B and leaving her to bring up her son alone. A son who had gone off to university and then moved on to a job in London and only came back to visit very rarely. She could feel that Anna had made the best of things and was able to make a viable living from the tourist accommodation, but Amy could sense the woman's loneliness beneath her practical and down to earth persona.

Amy could have decided to keep herself to herself, especially in view of the day that lay ahead, but compassion got the better of her and she invited Anna to share a coffee with her, and listened while Anna chatted away about previous visitors and her son's important job in a merchant bank in London.

Eventually it was time to go and Amy grabbed her notebook and laptop.

She had decided to walk the three-quarters of a mile or so to the Mill so that she could gather her thoughts and prepare herself. It was a perfect day, full of hope and promise, with daffodils and primroses filling the grass verges at the roadside. The single-track lane was quiet, and she had completed the whole stretch without meeting a vehicle or another pedestrian. She had telephoned ahead to tell them to expect her. Sam, Maggie and Catrin were all waiting by the doorway when she arrived.

She stood on the lane outside for a moment taking in the view of the Mill complex. The original stone building had been carefully restored with the Mill wheel still in place, although the fact that the water no longer ran through the mill race made it obvious that the mill was no longer in working order. There was a modern extension linking the main building to what must have originally been the grain-store but it had been done sympathetically in a way that enhanced the beauty of the original buildings.

Sam came forward to meet her and introduced her to his wife and his mother.

"You stayed in the village last night? You would have been more than welcome to stay here."

"Thank you," she said, "but I need to have somewhere I can escape to. Sometimes the sessions become very intense and I need to be able to switch off. It is always better if I only have contact with the 'presences' during the hours of daylight."

Sam led her into the modern extension which had been configured as a large central hallway, from which radiated four doors, two on each side. Two of them led back into the original mill building and provided two separate living units – one for Maggie, and one for Sam, Catrin and Emily. The two doors on the other side led to the original granary, which Sam explained had been converted to provide two holiday lets.

The entrance hall was large and well-proportioned, double height, with a vaulted ceiling of reclaimed oak beams. The floor had been re-laid with ancient slate flags, which she imagined had been sourced from reclamation yards. Some may even have come originally from the now disused quarry at the edge of the village, which she knew had been famous for its slate in the nineteenth century.

The lighting screamed 'industrial chic' with wall lights fashioned from pre-used Kilner jars, and a central pendant of glass and twisted copper wire. She guessed that Catrin, whose personality came across to her as extremely practical, had been the one who chose the light fittings.

On two sides of the room were oak pews, which appeared to have been pulled out of decommissioned chapels, strewn with multi-coloured cushions in vintage fabrics.

While Catrin's practicality suggested she had chosen the lighting, something about the softness of the fabrics used in the furnishings seemed more suited to Maggie's personality, she thought. She could feel that Maggie, although outwardly competent and doing her best to keep everyone else together, was in fact extremely sensitive and much less confident than she appeared to be.

On the opposite wall to the central doorway was a large oak dresser, littered with maps and leaflets of local attractions. In the centre of the room was a solid, almost black oak table whose thick legs still showed original axe marks. A cream lace runner stretched across the middle section and placed at each end were two matching enamel jugs, newly painted in a soft green, which held generous bunches of daffodils. As the entrance to a holiday complex it worked very well in terms of atmosphere, but as a place to commune with spirits, she was not quite so sure. The chapel pews especially might hold ghostly residues that could interfere with her task.

"We'll leave you to it, then," said Sam, "unless you would like a coffee to start with?"

"Oh, I'll take some time to get the feel of the place – I'll give you a knock when I want that coffee." She smiled at him, not wanting to appear too dismissive.

Almost as soon as he left the room, she was aware of flickering shadows, snatches of consciousness, fragments of memories. Then gradually, as she made sense of the impressions, she realised there were two main 'presences'. She could not see them physically but they were there in her mind – a thin, frail woman with lanky black hair and a frightened aspect, and a young boy about three years old who seemed strangely cheerful and at peace, given the circumstances. Presumably, it was the boy who had been in contact with Catrin's daughter, Emily. The woman's age was more difficult to determine. She had obviously suffered a great deal before her death, but Amy did not feel she was old, probably late teens or early twenties, she thought.

To begin with she decided to concentrate on the boy – he would be less demanding to deal with as he was already in contact with someone in the house.

"Why are you here?" She asked the boy, her mind focusing purely on him and ignoring the other shadow presences around her.

"I did not want to go with Mummy," the voice came clearly into her head. "I came back because Daddy was here, and I thought he might need me – but I could not seem to contact him and then he went too far away. I could not follow him there. But by then I had started to help Sarah. She has been here a long, long time, much longer than me. I knew she was here before, even before Mummy went away and tried to take me with her. So, I stayed here to try to help Sarah. She gets very confused and does not really know what is happening."

How kind he was, Amy thought, how sad that his life had been cut so short. She shook herself, feeling sorry for him would not get any of them very far.

She decided to make a start with the woman, although she was already very tired, perhaps she would just make contact and then leave the rest of the 'interview' for another day. She spent a few minutes 'introducing herself' to the female presence, putting her at ease and offering a place of safety for her to unburden herself. She would come back the following day and hopefully the woman would be able to trust her by then.

She went back to the kitchen in Maggie's part of the house. It was comfortable and homely, recently modernised but with a good old-fashioned solid fuel Rayburn warming the whole area.

Sam and Maggie were waiting for her but Catrin had taken Emily out for a walk in case the child was upset or disturbed by what Amy had to say. Catrin was still very sceptical about the whole idea of a medium and was worried in case it made things worse for the child.

Amy accepted the coffee and sandwiches they had prepared for her hungrily. It was surprising how much energy these interviews burned off. She did not feel she had been in the Mill a long time, but it was well past lunchtime when she went to report back to them.

"There's not much to tell at the moment, except that I have made contact…"

Sam started as if he did not quite believe what he was hearing.

"I've made contact," she repeated, "there seem to be two presences – your daughter's friend who seems to be a young boy, and a woman, but I think the woman has been here much longer than the little boy – I am not sure but when I feel her I seem to hear the name Sara or Sarah …? I will come back again tomorrow. I'll tell you more after my next session, when I hope I can help them both to move on."

Maggie gave a nervous laugh "You sound like a therapist."

"Well, in a way I suppose that is what I am."

* * * * * * * *

I thought I saw some sunlight today. It has been so long since that happened. I have been brooding in the darkness for so long now. A new lady came today, perhaps she brought in the light. It was just a brief glimpse of something other than this nothingness, but it lifted my heart. She said she wanted to help me. Can I trust her? I trust the boy, but he is so young. He gets mixed up as well as me. Can she really help me?

I have been so frightened – afraid of the miller, afraid of this place. For a long time, I did not want to remember. I just wanted to hide away in the darkness and grieve for my lost family. I tried to forget everything that had happened and lose myself in the shadows, but fractured memories returned to torment me. Now it is all beginning to come back to me.

The last thing I remember is the terribly cold weather. The winter had been long and hard, and the cart track was difficult to walk on as it was frozen and rutted from wagons and horses passing along it. I had been working at the Plas, but it was my afternoon off, and I was expected back home for tea. I was finding it more and more difficult to make progress along the track and I was pleased when I heard a wagon coming up behind me. I was not so pleased when I saw who it was. William Owens the miller. I had known him most of my life, but I did not like him at all. He was always sarcastic to me and made me feel uncomfortable. Still it was very cold, and the going was difficult so when he offered me a ride on the cart, I accepted. Perhaps he had a good side, I thought, and was trying in his own way to be kind.

I do not remember what happened after that. Only that I woke up with a dreadful headache and was lying on a damp slate floor with just the light of a single candle to see by. I can even remember what he said now – it is strange it is all becoming so clear now.

"Well, Lady Sarah, how do you like your new home. You'll be looking after me now, not those nobs at the Plas."

"*They will be looking for me ...*" *I whispered.*

"*Oh no, my lovely. I told your father I had seen you taking a short cut across the frozen lake, and that the ice had given way beneath you. I told him I had tried to rescue you but by the time I got near enough you had disappeared.*"

During the weeks that followed, I remember I tried to make my life better. I thought if I tried to please him, he might be kinder to me and in a way that did happen. All the while I was dreading what he might have in mind for me, what he wanted me there for, but apart from an occasional beating to keep me docile, he did not seem to want to touch me.

One day I had the beginnings of a plan.

"*I could cook for you Mr Owens. My father said I was a very good cook.*"

After that I was allowed up into the kitchen instead of being trapped down in the damp cellar, and we both had better food once I was cooking. I gradually began to feel stronger and I started thinking of ways to try to escape from this awful prison.

Things were better after I started cooking – because I was allowed into the kitchen I had a better idea of what he was doing – when he was going into the Mill or when he was going off in the cart for supplies. One day I was in luck – when he went out to the cart, he forgot to lock the kitchen door behind him. I waited until I heard the cart creaking its way out of the yard and then crept out of the kitchen door on to the yard.

Just as I thought I could really escape I heard again the rattle of the cart – he was coming back. He must have forgotten something, perhaps he realised he had not locked the door. I crept around the side of the Mill *and climbed on to a little footbridge that crossed the Mill Pond. I hoped from there I could peep out and see what was happening without being seen. I edged further along the slippery wooden planks, but the boards were half-rotten and slimy with lichen and moss. Suddenly I lost my footing and slid into the murky, freezing water of the pond.*

* * * * *

Anna was watching out for Amy when she got back to the B&B.

"How did you get on?"

"Oh, quite well really. I managed more than I thought I would. Today was just supposed to be to get the feel of what was going on, but I made more progress than I thought I would."

"What, exactly, is it you do," Anna was hesitant, not wanting to pry.

"I suppose the media would call me a 'ghost whisperer'" Amy shrugged. "I have always been clairvoyant, and I try to help when people have become stuck."

"Stuck?"

"Yes – I suppose that is the right description. When people pass over and the circumstances are confusing or unclear to them, sometimes they remain behind and need help to move on."

"So are there ghosts at the old Mill?"

"I think you will find there are ghosts nearly everywhere Anna," Amy said, softly. "It's just that not everyone is aware of them."

Anna was anxious: "Are there any ghosts here, in this house?"

Amy did not tell her of the old lady she had been vaguely aware of during her stay. A gentle woman in a flowered apron with a feather duster in her hand. The woman was no threat to anyone and seemed content enough to stay in the house undisturbed.

"Nothing for you to worry about," she reassured Anna. To change the subject, she continued:

"Have you lived in the village long?"

"About 20 years but I am a newcomer still really. I came here with my husband. He was born in the village but moved away to Liverpool for work, which was where I met him. He was made redundant a few years after we married, and we used his redundancy money to buy this place and run it as a B&B. It was ironic really because we had only been up and running for a couple of years when he died. My son helped me run it when he was a teenager, but after he finished college he moved to London for a work opportunity, so I have been running it on my own for a few years now."

"Do you feel settled here, then?"

"Oh yes, I love it really. I could not go back to Liverpool now. People seem to have two reactions when they move in here – either they don't realise how far away they are from the facilities in the nearest town and move away again within a year or two, or they feel that they have known the place before in some way and really bond here.

"The village used to be a lot busier than it is now," Anna continued. "In the 1900's there were two working quarries and a silver mine. The train used to take the slates and mineral ore down the valley to Shropshire and the Midlands. I think the place was quite cosmopolitan then, people moved in from all over to work in the mine and the quarries, and the village has retained this feeling of openness and welcome to all that is sometimes lacking in the smaller, more remote Welsh villages."

"So, you would not consider moving away again then?"

"No, I don't think anything would tempt me now. At least I know all my neighbours well now and if I need help as I get older, I dare say they will help me out. My son might even come back here one day, once he gets the London bug out of his system, but I doubt it somehow, unless he can find some well-paid employment locally."

"Perhaps he could set up an internet company?" Amy suggested, "He could work from anywhere then."

As she spoke, she had a vision of a youngish man sitting in a garden office working on a laptop. Maybe it would happen in the future, but maybe it would not.

Later that night Amy sat in her full-length cotton nightdress brushing her red-gold curls and staring into the dressing table mirror. She was glad she had deliberately chosen a newish B&B which did not have too much history. She needed a good night's sleep to cope with the following day. She drifted into a daydream and then became aware of Matthew.

"How's it going?" he asked gently.

"Oh, I'm making some progress – at least they came to me and did not hide themselves away."

"They need you. They need your help to set them free."

"Perhaps – but maybe I won't be able to do that."

"You can do it. You have more strength than you realise."

She smiled softly, longing for his physical presence once more, not just his emotional support.

"We'll see where I am tomorrow," she whispered into the mirror.

CHAPTER SEVENTEEN

As she took the small blue fabric holdall Maggie had lent her from the rear of the Suzuki and walked into the Mill entrance hall, Opal had the strangest feeling. Twenty-five years ago, she had carried her belongings through into the part of the building that belonged to Maggie and Paul.

The holdall contained the items Maggie had brought into the hospital ward for her and would see her through for a couple of days. Maggie had promised that she would take her to the cottage to pick up some more of her things as soon as she felt strong enough. She felt scruffy as she was wearing the same clothes she had been admitted in, which still showed signs of the fall. Her black denim jeans had been torn at the knee and her red floral shirt had been ripped as she slid down the stairs. Maggie had bought in some of her own clothes for her to wear but as Maggie was two sizes larger, Opal's only real option was to wear her own damaged ones.

"Maggie, it's so kind of you to bring me back here – are you sure I won't be in the way?"

"Not at all, it's the least we can do. We have spent the winter redecorating one of the holiday lets so we have not taken any bookings for that one yet, as we were not sure exactly when it would be finished. You can have all the privacy you want, but we will be nearby if you need anything."

Maggie had been so good. Coming to see her in hospital, and now bringing her back here to the Mill. She remembered the place quite clearly, although there had been several alterations since the days when Steve and Ellie, Maggie and Paul, had all lived there, and she had helped Steve with his recording in the music studio.

The cottage Maggie showed her into had been part of the original storage barn and had been linked to the main building by a contemporary double storey extension. The two ancient buildings linked by a very modern addition sounded as if it should not work but somehow it did and the resulting façade, softened in front of the old stone walls with flower-planted troughs, looked attractive and welcoming.

Her part of the complex led via a corridor from the central entrance area, past the back of the other holiday let which appeared to be occupied. There was a spacious living room/kitchen on the ground floor and two small double bedrooms and a bathroom on the first. Everything looked wonderful as it had all been prepared ready for the season – fresh pale green emulsion on the walls, new bedding, and curtains in ivory with a flower-sprigged design. She felt she would not be able to stay here long as it was all ready for paying guests and Maggie and Sam would want to make the most of the season. As soon as she felt a little stronger, she would go back to her rental in the village, which she had originally booked for two months. At least at the Mill, she felt she would have some protection from Paul.

Thinking about Paul again made her shudder. She had not told the police what happened. She did not really think she was in any danger now, especially not staying here with Maggie, Sam and Catrin all close at hand, but the thought of seeing him again made her feel extremely uncomfortable.

She still could not understand why he had wanted to see her so badly – even if what he had told Ellie had sent her over the edge, she had been very unhappy for a long while before. Surely, he did not think he bore the sole responsibility for what happened – or did he? Was that why he was so worried about the others finding out? Was he frightened to admit to himself that he had caused the tragedy?

She had asked Maggie if anyone had heard from Paul at all, since her fall.

"He's been sending text messages to Sam, asking how you are – I think he has been trying to find out if the police are looking for him. You should really think about telling them, you know. What he did was way out of order."

"Yes, I know but ..." the thought of making statements and all that would involve just upset her more. Better to leave things as they were. It could have been an accident after all, although Maggie had told her all about his temper.

Opal unpacked the few bits and pieces Maggie had brought for her from the borrowed holdall and then went to look for her again.

Maggie looked up from preparing lunch when Opal walked in. "Do you think you will be comfortable over there?"

Opal nodded, "You've made it really nice, Maggie. Its far posher than the place I am renting in the village."

"We'll have some lunch and then, when you're ready I'll pop you back there so that you can pick up a few more clothes and things."

"That would be great, Maggie, but I don't want to stay here more than a couple of days or so until I feel a bit stronger. You will be losing money on the holiday rental if I am staying here."

"You take as much time as you need Opal. To be honest we did not think we would have had that part of the building redecorated as quickly as we did, and we haven't even started trying to market it for this season yet."

Opal felt they had been talking about her situation for long enough, it was time to change the subject.

"So, what has been happening with your visitor?" she asked. Maggie had told her about the proposed visit by Amy Rae, although Opal did not really understand why they had called her in. Most children had invisible friends at some time or other when they were small, she thought, although she could not remember having one herself. Perhaps they all forget about it once they are older, she decided.

Maggie shrugged: "Well, I don't quite know what to make of her at all. She isn't at all what you might expect."

"Not like Madame Arcarty in Blithe Spirit then?" Opal managed to joke, despite her worries about Paul.

Maggie laughed "Not at all. She is young, well, mid-twenties I suppose, which is young as far as we are concerned, and very modern somehow, not at all what you might imagine. She came to see us yesterday and is with Sam and Catrin now, I think. But you will meet her later I expect. She is staying in the village but came back again this morning while I was fetching you from the hospital. She says she must do some more 'research' into what is happening here. In fact, by tonight I hope we might have some definite answers – this situation is just so unsettling, and we are all so worried about the effect it is having on young Emily."

* * * * *

After their visit to pick up more of Opal's belongings Maggie settled her back into the holiday let so that she could have a sleep. She had told Maggie that her head was still feeling woozy and Maggie urged her not to try to get better too soon but to rest as much as she could.

On returning to her kitchen, Maggie put the kettle onto the Rayburn and began to think about everything Opal had told her, both in the hospital and on the drive home. How had she put up with Paul all those years? He had always bullied her and put her down, telling her she was useless. Even before he had started physically hurting her, the emotional abuse had been there.

She remembered that after Ellie had died, she had applied for a part-time job as an Admin Assistant at the local veterinary practice. It was a way of trying to divert her mind from the grief and guilt that followed.

Sam had been settled in school by then, and she had felt that it would be good to get away from the Mill for a few hours a week. Paul had his library job in Chester to go off to every day, but she was constantly surrounded by all the memories and the thought that they could have done so much more to prevent the tragedy. Paul had been totally derisory. "They will never give that job to you – you've been away from mainstream work for too long, buried away here. You don't stand a chance."

Luckily, she had already submitted her application or what he said might have stopped her. His words so often did affect her actions and made her doubt herself and her abilities. She could not understand why he seemed to always put her down. Sometimes she felt she was going mad. There were times when she regained the ability to push back and assert herself, but sometimes she just felt too tired to do anything other than just give in. She vividly remembered one morning before Sam was born going into their bedroom to tidy up while Paul was at work. As she walked through the open door, a voice suddenly came into her head, so strongly that she nearly fell over:

"What the hell are you doing here with this man?"

She had never understood where it came from. Was it her dead grandmother looking out for her, or was it her subconscious warning her of trouble ahead? She had never been able to work out the source of the voice, but she often wished she had paid it more attention before Sam came along.

Regarding the job application, she did get an interview, much to her surprise, and four weeks later started work at the vet's practice three days a week. The hours fitted well with Sam's schooling and she found herself really enjoying it – even if some of the patients that came into the surgery had heart-breaking outcomes. It was good to feel that she could make a difference, could help with frightened animals, and tearful owners.

Perhaps that was the beginning of her realisation that Paul was toxic for her. She was now earning some money quite independently of the financial set-up at the Mill and having a role of her own gave her far more confidence. Perhaps Paul sensed he was losing control of her, and maybe that was the reason his temper seemed to get so much worse, and he started to become violent.

On the second occasion that he had hit her, she decided that enough was enough. She had consulted Citizen Advice and then a local solicitor and buoyed by their reactions had found the courage to tell Paul to move out. The divorce that followed was painful and difficult, but Maggie was amazed by the amount of help and support she had from the local community.

Finances had been the sticking point, but that was why so little work had been done on the Mill project until Sam had been old enough to help. He had been seeing Catrin since they were both 16, and at 20 she had moved in with him. The year after Emily was born, they had finally formalised things and Maggie was delighted to have such a supportive daughter-in-law.

Paul's salary from the library enabled him to get a mortgage on a small cottage half way between the Mill and his workplace in Chester, and he still kept in close touch with Sam, much as Maggie hated the idea of him having any influence at all with their son.

Maggie made a black coffee and decided she had spent far too long thinking about Paul and how everything had gone wrong between them. It was time to think about the future and to start living her life again instead of hiding away in the past. She hoped that the visit of Amy might help them all to move forward, although if all it did was relieve Sam's mind about Emily's 'friend' that would be an achievement of its own.

* * * * *

Amy's second day went better than expected. The woman called Sarah had already remembered a lot of her story after her brief talk with Amy the day before. She was obviously trying to help herself. She told Amy what had happened to her. The miller had kidnapped her and kept her a prisoner until one day she had tried to escape. When he came home unexpectedly, she had panicked and fallen into the Mill pond. She then added the final piece of the puzzle.

"Suddenly it was as if I was outside my body looking down on what was happening. I saw the cart pull up and the mill owner rush over to the pond. He must have heard the splash when I fell into it, and I suppose I must have cried out in shock. He stood for a while looking down into the dark depths of the pool. He went away, it seemed for a long time, but then came back with a rope and pulled out what looked like a sodden bundle of rags. With a huge shock I realised it must be my body. He loaded it on to the cart and drove round to the old stable block. I followed him somehow still looking down from above and I saw him bury my remains under the dirt floor of the old stables."

Amy Rae sat quietly, trying to sooth the distress that the woman's memories were causing.

"Now you know – now you remember – do you think you can accept what happened and move on, move away from this place? You know it is time for you to go, now that you know what has happened to you? If you can move on, then I think Tristan will be able to go to – I think you will both be free to leave this place. Just look towards the light, follow the light and you will be free."

"I can see it – I can see the light. It has come for me – to take me away from all this darkness and despair."

Suddenly Amy was aware of a great sense of relief, a melting away of all the grief and horror. She felt, or at least hoped, that she had done her job.

Amy did not join Sam and the others for supper that evening – she felt too exhausted.

"I don't think you will have any more trouble now," she told Catrin, Sam and Maggie. "I think we should leave things to settle down for a week or so. I will ring you then and if you are happy, I will send you my bill then."

"Wouldn't you like us to settle your expenses now though," offered Catrin, "what about your costs at the B&B?"

"No, its fine. I want to know you are happy with the results before I start charging you. I have a business to build and I need to build it on goodwill. I don't want people accusing me of being a fake medium or anything like that."

"Well if you are sure," Catrin could see what she meant. When dealing with matters of the paranormal it was difficult to know who was real and who was just preying on the credulous.

"There is just one more thing," Maggie hesitated to mention it. "I don't know if you can do anything about this one as it all happened a long time ago."

"Tell me."

"Well it was my father – he died in an accident at a tube station, years and years ago when I was still in my teens. What was odd though was the tube station was nowhere near his usual route to and from work, and I have always wondered what he was doing there."

"Have you got an item that belonged to him, something I could use to contact him perhaps?"

Maggie ran up to her bedroom and found the gold watch that she had always kept in her jewellery box as a memento of her father.

"Will this do?"

"That will be fine – although I can't make any promises. I will take it away with me and let you know if I get anywhere."

CHAPTER EIGHTEEN

After Amy had left them, Sam checked his messages. Three missed calls and a text from his dad. He was still finding it hard to come to terms with everything he was learning about the past, but he knew he would have to catch up with Paul sometime. It would be only fair to hear his side of the story. His mother was bound to see the worst side of Paul's behaviour.

He rang back and arranged to meet Paul on the following Sunday, and then went back into Maggie's kitchen to talk about Amy's visit.

The kitchen was in turmoil when he entered.

"We can't find Emily," his mum turned to him anxiously, "have you seen any sign? She and Mindy were playing in the walled courtyard at the back, and I only checked on them a few minutes ago, but they have both gone now! I thought the back gate was secure, but they must have found a way out somehow."

"Well we'd better all start looking now," Sam strode outside, as the others followed and started calling for her.

Just then they heard excited barking from the far end of the yard by the semi-derelict stable block. They rushed across and Mindy came running to meet them. Emily stood by the threshold, just inside the stable door.

"Trissi told me to come," she explained. "He said he had to go away now but he said we need to dig under the floor here."

Maggie, Sam and Catrin stood frozen in shock. What was the child saying now?

"Well," said Maggie, "She was right about looking under the bed for Ellie's diary."

* * * * *

The following Sunday Sam and Paul met up in the village and took the two dogs, Sam's Jack Russell Mindy, and Paul's black lab Bonny, on the popular trek over the mountain to the top of the waterfall. One of the seven wonders of Wales, with the highest single-drop waterfall in Britain, Pistyll Rhaeadr was a place Maggie and Sam recommended their visitors to visit, either on foot, or on the longer route around by car.

The first mile was usually busy with dog walkers who came out from as far away as Birmingham, but this early in the morning most of the visitors had yet to arrive and their walk was quiet as they made their way up past the old quarry. The path was slippery with wet slate chippings to begin with, but then turned to grass, and up on the top of the mountain were boggy areas spikey with rushes, and muddy dips to be avoided.

As they walked Paul asked Sam how Opal was.

"Oh, I think she's recovering okay. She is out of hospital now and staying with Mum for a bit. She's booked a cottage for a few weeks, but she doesn't feel strong enough to go back there just yet."

"I didn't mean for her to fall, Sam, I hope you know that."

"I'm not sure whether she really blames you or not. I don't think she wants to involve the police though."

Paul shook his head.

"I got so worried about what she would tell everyone. I just lost it somehow. I pushed past her on the way out and that was when it happened. I saw her in a heap at the bottom of the stairs and she seemed unconscious. I panicked and rushed out of the house without checking whether she was alive or not – I was frightened of what I might find, I suppose – but I called the ambulance on my mobile straight away and then watched from a distance to make sure someone did come and find her as soon as possible. I didn't dare go back into the house in case she was actually dead."

"Well apparently, she just had bruises and a slight concussion, so it could have been much worse. She did not seem to remember much about your visit – only that you were there and did not want her to tell the rest of us something only she knew."

"It's all such a mess, Sam. I suppose I have been living with guilt about Ellie all these years. I thought that it was my talk with her the night before she died that made her do it."

"That may be, Dad, but Mum feels guilty too. Everyone seems to think it was their fault somehow, even Opal."

"Did your Mum tell you the other thing?"

"About you not being my real Dad? Yes – it was a shock, but I have been thinking things through. Just because you are not my biological dad, it does not stop me still thinking about you as Dad. You were the one who helped to bring me up after all. Even after you and Mum split up you were always still there for me. You played football with me and took me to Cubs and later Scouts and encouraged me to do all that kind of stuff. And you took me away for weekend camps, just the two of us, so we could have real time together."

"I'm so glad you see it like that Sam. That was one of the things I did not want Opal to tell, my doubts about you being my biological son."

The dogs were running ahead now, playing with each other, and stopping to sniff at rabbit holes. The day was bright and clear, not too hot, but ideal for walking, and the view from the top of the mountain was stunning with its patchwork of fields below and the little villages and hamlets dotted over the landscape.

Sam felt it was time to change the subject and started to tell Paul about the visit by Amy Rae. Paul was quite shocked.

"You mean to say that because of this girl's visit you found a body in the old stable block that had been there for decades?"

"I know – it seems unbelievable doesn't it? The body was just a collection of rags and bones, really, but there was one thing of interest – among the bones was a silver chain with a letter S on it. Amy Rae said she thought the woman she spoke to was called Sarah. We've arranged for the body to be properly buried in the churchyard near the grave of Ellie and Tristan."

Before they knew it, Paul and Sam reached the top of the waterfall and were peering down at the natural stone bridge that spanned it, watching the torrent as it fell into the pool below. The waterfall was impressive, swollen from the early Spring rains, and poured in cataracts around the rocks on the way down. From the top its famous long drop of 240ft looked even higher and the cascade hit the pool in spectacular explosions of spray. Just as they were gazing down, amazed at the power and strength of the flow of water, Bonny ran to sniff at a rabbit hole close to the cliff edge. Paul went nearer to call her back, slipped on the wet grass and slid over the edge.

Sam's heart almost stopped beating and he was afraid to look over the edge, scared of what he might see. When he did look just seconds later, although it felt far longer, it was not quite as bad as he thought. Paul had fallen onto a rough ledge about 30ft below. He was conscious and moving, but his leg was twisted awkwardly beneath him and his moaning was laced with the occasional curse.

"Stupid bloody dog!" was all that Sam could make out.

"Stay still Dad. I am calling for help now. Try not to move too much just in case."

Sam was worried that the ledge might be fragile or slippery and his Dad could still fall to his death. At least his mobile was in signal – reception could be very patchy up in the mountains - and he was able to make the emergency call straight away.

The wait for help seemed to go on for ever, but it was probably only about an hour. Sam had put the two dogs back on their leads as he did not want to have to worry about them as well. The terrain was difficult for emergency vehicles to navigate but eventually he heard sirens making their way up the valley road beneath, along the lane that led to the foot of the falls. There was no proper track up to the top but eventually a Mountain Rescue Land Rover scrambled its way through the surrounding fields and up to the top. With difficulty the mountain rescue team winched Paul up to the 4x4 which then made its way back down to the waiting ambulance below.

*****

Two days later, Maggie found herself driving to the hospital in Shrewsbury yet again, this time to see Paul for afternoon visiting. Sam had told her about the talk they had had on the way to the waterfall and had been to visit Paul the previous night.

"He wants to talk to you Mum. He wants to try to put things right between you."

"I don't think there's much chance of that Sam, but I will go and see him," she had reluctantly agreed.

The countryside was looking at its brightest best: the fields recovering from their winter mud baths, and fresh greenery on the trees and hedges glowing in the early afternoon sunlight.

She found Paul's bed easily enough – he was in the next ward from the one Opal had occupied only a few days before.

"Thank you for coming Maggie," he looked genuinely pleased to see her.

"Sam said you wanted to talk to me," she sat down at his bedside, arms folded across her chest in a protective gesture. She still felt uncomfortable in his presence, almost threatened somehow, although she felt she should listen to what he had to say. She was suddenly aware of how much he had aged over the years since their divorce. His hair was almost completely grey now and his face was lined and drawn, crumpled with worry lines. They had had to meet socially on several occasions over the last few years, but she had never really taken the time to look at him properly, avoiding eye contact whenever she could.

"I've made such a mess of everything Maggie. These last few days have brought it all home to me. How badly I treated you, how I allowed my temper to cause Opal's fall, how I am at least partly to blame for what happened with Ellie and Tristan."

"Well, I think we can all share the blame for Ellie's actions Paul. It wasn't just down to you, and Steve has to take some of the blame too."

"I probably made everything worse though. And I treated you appallingly. It was only after we split up that I realised what I had thrown away. These last few days I have had time to do a lot of thinking, and I want to try and make things better. I have really missed you during these years we have been apart. I did not realise how important you were to me until we broke up."

Maggie listened with interest. She had always felt it strange that Paul had not had any other serious relationships (at least as far as she knew) but she could not believe he regretted their divorce. Their breakup was something she had felt as a total relief at the time, although she, too, had somehow been unable to get on with her life. She knew one thing for certain though, Paul would never be allowed back into her life in the way he had been before.

"I don't think we could ever have a full relationship again Paul," she told him. "There is no way I could go back to that. But we can at least be friends, if only for Sam's sake."

"Sam means so much to me Maggie. I thought I would lose him if he found out I was not his real Dad.

I had behaved so badly to you I thought he would leap at the chance to disown me, but he still calls me Dad. I am so proud of the lad, and he made sure I got the help I needed as quickly as possible. He's got a cool head, that one, - a good lad to have around in a crisis."

"You don't need to tell me that," Maggie smiled. "How are you feeling now Paul?"

"I was incredibly lucky. I could have fallen the whole way down and I would not have survived that. My leg was broken, and I have a few crushed ribs, but really things could have been so much worse. That is why I have been doing so much thinking about the past. I feel I've been given a second chance – a chance to put right some of the things I did wrong before."

"I'm glad you see it that way Paul. I would be happy for you to come and visit us all at the Mill now, but I cannot promise any more than that now. The past is still too painful for me."

Chapter Nineteen

A week later, while calling for the milk and papers in the village, Maggie met Roy the postman once again.

"Hi Maggie, I've a package here for a Ms Opal Graham, but the place it's addressed to is all shut up. Someone said she might be staying with you?"

Oh, the joys of rural life, thought Maggie. Nothing ever got past the locals. Still, surely that was better than the stories one heard of people lying dead and undiscovered for weeks in cities, with no-one even noticing they were missing.

Back at the Mill she handed the package straight to Opal.

"It's from my mother," Opal said, guiltily. "My phone broke in the fall and I have never been in touch to tell her what happened. At first, I did not want to worry her and then with all the excitement that has been going on since, it just completely went out of my mind. She says she tried to ring me to tell me what she was sending but could not get through!"

"So, what has she sent you then?"

Opal starts to leaf through the enclosures to her mother's brief covering note.

"Well there's a letter here from my birth dad's solicitors in Jamaica. Apparently, he died last year and has left me a small inheritance. They want me to get in touch with them so I will have to do that soon I suppose. The other documents ......" Opal paused suddenly.

"I think I'll take these to my room, if you don't mind Maggie, it's all a lot to take in. I'll pop back after supper and tell you all about it."

* * * * *

Catrin was delighted to hear from Amy when she rang in May. By then Emily was no longer talking about her friend Trissi. In fact, Catrin had asked her daughter if she had seen him lately, as she was a bit concerned in case Emily was upset by his absence.

"Oh, no, he told me he had to go away. He hasn't been here for a long time, not since he told me to go to the stables."

"Does it make you sad that he went away?"

"No, not really. He was happy to be going – he did not tell me where, but he wanted to go there. I do miss him a little bit, but I have all my friends at school to talk to now, so I don't need him as much."

Catrin felt she should be happy with this result and leave things as they were. With any luck in a few months Emily would have forgotten all about her 'imaginary friend'.

The previous day Sam had come home from a farm visit with a ginger kitten for Emily.

"It might help to take her mind off all of this," he had explained to Catrin.

"Well, we'll just have to make sure Mindy doesn't eat him!"

They had watched the interaction between the kitten and the curious Jack Russell a little anxiously, laughing when it became apparent that the dog was frightened of the new arrival.

Sam had previously rung Amy to tell her about the discovery in the stables. She had not been surprised in view of what Sarah had told her. Sam explained what had happened after they had found the bones.

"We've arranged for Sarah's body to be removed and buried in the churchyard at Pennant, in a plot near to that occupied by Ellie and Tristan. We still do not know who she was but Catrin's Aunt Delyth is convinced that she was a relation from several generations back. I do not know if we can ever find anything to prove that. We did find a silver chain with the body, inscribed with the initial 'S', so it could possibly be the Sarah that Delyth keeps talking about."

Catrin told Amy that everything seemed to have settled down at the Mill. Amy had not mentioned all the other shadowy fragments that she had been aware of whilst she spent time there, but if these were not causing any concern to the living occupants, best to let well alone.

"I'll send you my bill then. By the way, I do not know whether you will want to tell Maggie this or not. I will leave it up to you. But I did find out why her father was at that particular tube station. Apparently, he had a mistress, a former secretary, whom he had set up in a little flat near Paddington station and he would visit every Thursday afternoon. His office thought he was consulting the firm's solicitor, but in fact he was spending time with Rosemary Lloyd.

"In fact, he had been making plans and if not for that fatal accident he was going to tell the family about Rosemary, and probably move in with her. The accident occurred when he was actually on his way home to talk to his family about it..."

Catrin finished the phone call deep in thought. Perhaps it would be kinder to tell Maggie that Amy Rae had been unable to make contact.

It did give her cause to wonder. She had heard so much about Ellie's hero worship of her father. If he had left the family, had left his little princess, and betrayed her then, would that have made a difference to the outcome? Would she have learnt earlier on in life how to cope when things went wrong?

One thing was becoming clear to her though – Maggie, Opal, Paul, Steve – all of them felt guilt for what had happened to Ellie and Tristan. How much of that guilt was justified and how much down to the fact that Ellie had been unable to deal with cold, hard reality? She had obviously been mentally ill at the time and not responsible for her actions.

* * * * *

After supper Opal knocked tentatively on Maggie's kitchen door.

"I thought I would just let you know about my package."

Maggie looked at her anxiously. Opal's eyes were still red, and it looked as if she had been crying for ages.

"Are you okay, Opal?"

"Yes, I'm happy really, Maggie. It is just that things are quite different from what I had always thought. My real father did not seem to be interested in me. He had come to visit and gave me this pendant" she fingered the chain around her neck, "when I was seventeen but then

I never heard from him again and I thought he had forgotten all about me. But apparently when he came to visit, and saw I was so well looked after by my mum and stepfather, he did not want to unsettle me by coming back into my life permanently. He had made my mother promise not to tell me, but he had been writing to her regularly, asking about me. Now that he is dead, she felt she no longer needed to honour that promise and she thought I should know that he had been asking about me all these years."

Opal's tears started to fall once again, but she was not sure whether she was happy or sad.

* * * * *

"It's so peaceful here, Sam," Maggie reached out to touch his hand. They were sitting in the churchyard as the sun gradually sank down behind the small church and its surrounding hills, and the swallows swooped above in the turquoise, pink and grey sky, scooping up the evening insects.

"Do you think they are at peace now?" Sam nodded towards the nearby grave, with its neatly tended grass and fresh floral tribute. The names of Ellie and Tristan were chiselled on the marble headstone. Close by was the fresh mound where Sarah's body now rested but there was no stone yet to mark it, and until they knew her identity for sure it was difficult to know what they could put on any stone.

Sam and Maggie had bought flower bulbs to plant on each of the graves, daffodils and crocuses for Ellie and Tristan, and snowdrops for Sarah.

"I hope so, Sam. I hope Amy Rae has helped Tristan to move on, and finding Sarah's remains perhaps has given her some peace."

"What about you Mum – have you found any peace?"

"I don't feel quite as guilty as I did Sam. For years I thought it was all my fault and I suppose in a way it was."

"No, Mum – it wasn't your fault. Ellie had a choice. Okay, so she had had problems and upsets in her life, but so have we all. We do not just go and hide away as she did. We learn how to deal with things."

"Quite the expert are you Sam?" his mum laughed. "You haven't had too much trauma to deal with yet, have you?"

"Maybe not, Mum, but I hope I would never hurt the people around me the way that Ellie did. Look what she did to you – ruined your life for years."

"Perhaps you are right, Sam. But I still think it was Ellie's illness that caused her to do what she did. And I worry that I did not realise how desperate she felt."

"You've always done your best Mum. After Paul left, you brought me up all on your own, and I can't say I've got any moans."

"Was it a dreadful shock Sam, when I told you about Steve?"

"No, strangely enough, it wasn't really. Paul and I were always so different somehow, although to give him his due he did spend a lot of time with me, even more after the two of you separated. I think he was frightened of losing touch with us all."

CHAPTER TWENTY

"There's someone I want you to meet Maggie," Bill Jenkins, Chairman of the Village Show, came over to her while she was counting the takings from the Coffee Morning Fundraiser.

"This is Mike Lane; he's just moved back to the area and he wants to help with the village show."

Maggie looked up and saw a tall, pleasant-looking man, with well-cut silver hair and round, silver-rimmed glasses.

Mike Lane? – the name rang a bell.

"Hello, Mike, good to meet you. Your name is familiar somehow – did you used to live around here once before then?"

"Yes, I spent several years here – but it was over 20 years ago now. I used to work as a counsellor at the surgery."

Maggie stared at him, cold shivers running through her. It was so strange, all these events coming now, all the mysteries around Ellie's death becoming clearer.

"Do you remember my sister Ellie then?" she asked.

"I do, very clearly," he hesitated. "In fact, she was the reason I decided to stop counselling and try another branch of medicine instead. If you like we can talk about it sometime – it is a bit too painful, and a bit too public, to discuss it here."

Maggie shook his hand, gratefully.

"I would like that very much Mike – would you like to come out to the Mill one evening or we could meet in the hotel in the village?"

"Perhaps the hotel would be best," Mike suggested. "How about a week tonight, 7.30?"

Maggie thought that the week would never pass. She was so anxious to find out what her sister's thinking had been. Once some of the questions were answered maybe they could all get on with their lives.

She had asked Opal to go with her to the meeting. If she found it all too much to cope with, it would help to have some moral support. Opal had decided to stay on in the area and arranged to take the holiday let on a longer tenancy, which suited the owner as it provided a more continuous occupancy during the autumn and winter months.

Opal had also started to help out as a volunteer at the school Catrin taught at, and was busy learning Welsh as half the pupils at the school had Welsh as their first language, although there were others who only spoke English.

Maggie left her car at Opal's rented cottage, and the two women walked down to the hotel. Maggie was glad of a chance to catch up.

"Did you hear anymore from your father's lawyers?"

"Yes, I rang them last week. Apparently, Wesley had been living with a lady called Rosa for ten years and the house and most of his estate went to her, but the residue was bequeathed to me."

"Yes, I remember you said something about a small bequest."

"Well, it wasn't really that small. It amounts to about £20,000 but I will have to wait a while for the money to come through."

"Gosh, that's a nice surprise. What will you do with it?"

"I haven't really decided yet, but I might use it for a holiday to go and see my Jamaican roots perhaps. I had thought of taking my mother, but she is getting a bit frail now. It may be too much for her to manage."

"Is she on her own now?"

"Yes, my step-father died last year just before my cancer scare. I think the two events coming so close to together made her health more fragile. If I am planning to make my life here, which seems more and more likely, I might try and bring her up here where I can keep a better eye on her. I rang her last night and had a long chat. Apparently, she had been wanting to tell me that my father was still in touch for many years, but he insisted he did not want to endanger my happiness here."

Opal still felt tearful at the thought. For so many years now, she had given up on her father, because she felt he had abandoned her, but now it turned out he had been trying to look out for her all that time. Her mother had explained that he had stopped helping financially when Opal was a baby because he had got in with a bad crowd and had gone to prison for several years. When he came out, he had resolved to sever all ties with the people who had got him into trouble, and had gone off touring in various places around the world until he had got himself sorted out. At the time he contacted her when she was seventeen, he had got his life back on track, but by then he felt it was too late to become involved in her life.

"It's a sad story," Maggie gave her a quick hug.

"It is, but at least I now know that he did care about me. So really you could say I have been lucky – I had three parents all trying to do their best for me!"

"Were you really upset when he did not contact you after he gave you that pendant?"

"I was a bit, but Mum had warned me that he probably would not stay around for long, so I suppose I just made the best of it, knowing I could rely on Mum and Justin to be there for me."

* * * * *

Mike was already there when they arrived at the hotel, standing at the bar with a glass of wine in his hand.

"What will you ladies have?"

Maggie asked for her usual tonic and lime as she was driving, but Opal chose orange juice. Her head still did not feel as if it could handle much alcohol after her concussion, although it had been several months since the accident.

They chose a small table in the window of the lounge, tucked away from the diners in the larger part of the room.

There were several holidaymakers laughing and chatting noisily near the bar, which meant they could talk freely without being overheard.

"I did try to find you after Ellie died," Maggie told him.

"I had moved away, and I did not hear what had happened for a while. My wife had been diagnosed with an aggressive cancer that needed intensive treatment, and I had arranged to rent a flat near the hospital in Birmingham while she was an in-patient. It took a long time, but she did eventually recover. I managed to get a job working in cancer support in the same hospital so that worked out very well, but it meant I never came back to the surgery. We had been saving up to buy a house around here, but after Janey's illness we used the money to buy a property near the hospital.

"Dr Andrew did get in touch finally to tell me what had happened. I think he wanted to keep it from me until my wife's treatment was showing signs of progress, but by then the post mortem and inquest had passed and it was too late for me to add anything to the findings.

"I had already decided that counselling was far too dangerous for me to practice. I do not want to make excuses, but because I was so worried about my wife, I did not notice how fixated Ellie was becoming about me. I think she was fantasising about us having a life together, although I am sure I never gave her any encouragement. She seemed to take my interest in her case, as personal interest in her, although I did try to point out that I was just doing my job.

"She called me the day it happened and asked to meet me. I knew it would be a mistake, but she sounded so desperate. I drove out to meet her and told her that there was no way she would have a future with me, and that I could no longer counsel her, but that was obviously the last straw as far as she was concerned. I went back to the surgery that day and arranged for Dr Andrew to ask a colleague of mine to help her but by then it was too late.

"I know she had other problems too, but I think if I had handled things better and used the sessions differently things would have had a more positive outcome. It frightened me, to be honest, how much she had woven fantasies around me, in such a short time."

"Knowing Ellie, I suppose that all makes perfect sense," said Maggie, and Opal nodded in agreement. They could both easily see how Ellie could have become dependent on someone she saw as an escape route from a less than perfect life.

"How is your wife now?" Opal asked.

"She passed away three years ago," Mike replied. "She did recover from the initial cancer, and we had quite a good life together for many years, but she was never as strong afterwards. I think the treatment that killed the cancer had taken its toll on her body, and she seemed very frail afterwards. She finally succumbed to pneumonia after a bout of flu. It was heart-breaking at the time, but I am beginning to get my life back together now. I thought moving back here would be a fresh start, but I knew I had to put the experience with Ellie behind me.

"I really needed to have this conversation as much as you Maggie."

Chapter Twenty-One

"Sam, time is getting on now, and I'm going to have to let Sylvie know definitely how many of us are coming down for Caroline's wedding. I did send a provisional reply saying the three of us were hoping to come, but I need to tell her definitely now. Have you had a chat with Catrin about it?"

"Well, she's not that keen on going, to be honest Mum. She is still struggling with morning sickness now. This pregnancy is completely different from when she had Emily. She sailed through that one, but this time she is finding it a lot harder. The doctors have told her not to overdo things as it is still early days yet. She's cut down her teaching to two days a week but she may even have to stop that if she doesn't start to feel better soon, but at least the summer holidays are coming up so she will be able to rest more then. As long as she doesn't go too mad on preparing lessons – she can get very driven at times!"

"Poor Catrin, I could tell she was suffering. You won't want to leave her now, though, will you Sam?"

"Not really Mum, but I don't want to let you down if you want to go."

"Well, I have thought of a plan if you would rather not come with me – I did mention it to Mike, and he would be happy to keep me company if you would rather stay here."

"Mike? Do you know him that well now then Mum? Are you sure about this?"

"Oh yes, I'm sure I would him like to come with me. I will ring Sylvie and ask if it will be okay to bring him instead of you and Catrin. I'm sure they won't mind."

* * * * *

The mellow September sun streaming through the bedroom window woke Maggie just before her alarm was set to go off.

The wedding was not until 1 o'clock but they would need a good breakfast to see them through as they would be lucky to eat at the reception before about 5, if previous experience were anything to go by. She turned to Mike, lying by her side, but he was already wide awake. She wondered if he was having misgivings. She was rather throwing him in the deep end as far as meeting her family was concerned.

The two of them had called at Sylvie's home for a drink and nibbles the night before, but had not stayed long as Sylvie and Tom were still up to their eyes in wedding arrangements and there was a constant stream of visitors to the house. She had managed to introduce Mike to them though, and he seemed quite at ease talking to them.

"How do you feel this morning?" she asked him, rubbing his arm affectionately.

"Oh, I'm fine. I can't say weddings are really my favourite thing, but I am glad I will be there to support you."

"Yes, thank you so much. I would have felt a bit out of it if I had come on my own and, although Sam had offered to come with me, I know he didn't want to leave Catrin at the moment."

"How many months is she now?"

"The baby is due in late January/early February – so she is about 5 months gone. I'm surprised she is still having morning sickness now, but some poor women apparently have it the whole time."

"That's the only thing I regret about my marriage to Janey," he confided. "We had decided to leave trying for a family until we were more settled, and had bought our own home here, but then her illness got in the way of all that. I wish we could have had a child. A daughter would have been nice, to carry on something of Janey for the future, but it was not to be," he sighed.

"Paul and I had our problems," Maggie admitted, "but I would not have missed having Sam for anything. He has been such a rock, especially the last few years."

Mike felt it was time to change the subject, before they both became too melancholy, thinking of the past.

"Isn't it time we went down to breakfast?"

* * * * *

As they sat in the attractive, modern Catholic church, with its pretty, contemporarily designed, stained glass windows, Maggie was so glad she had asked Mike to come with her. It was a bit of a risk, she knew. They had not known each other very long at all. Since the meeting in the hotel with Opal, they had met twice for drinks, and then several times for dinner in town. True, the dinners in town had led on to overnight stays at Mike's cottage but this wedding was a little different. It was a statement that they were a real couple, not just part of a casual relationship.

They had booked into a small private guest house in Brentwood not far from the church where Caroline was getting married and arranged a taxi to take them to the church a few miles away. Sylvie's family were not particularly religious but Caroline's fiancé, Simon, was the son of a couple who had moved over from Ireland before he was born, and the family had kept up their spiritual tradition.

The church was nearly full when they arrived.

"No wonder they could not include the guests' children as well," Maggie told Mike, after they had been shown to a pew on the bride's side of the church.

"But there's a baby over there, and a couple of toddlers two aisles away."

"I suppose those must the children of close relatives – they could not very well ban them I suppose. It is a pity they could not have more kids here really. Some people find children at services disruptive, but I always think churches are exactly the place for children to be, to make it a real family thing."

The bride only kept them waiting a few minutes and looked truly radiant. A pretty girl when dressed casually, in her simple full-length ivory silk dress, and with a short veil attached to a comb in her chestnut hair, she looked stunning. The ivory dress showed off her clear skin and deep blue eyes to perfection.

As the service proceeded Maggie found herself examining her own faith. She would almost have liked to embrace the whole Catholic ideology – it seemed so safe somehow. Pray, repent, and you will not have to worry about anything or anyone you care for as they will be looked after. But she knew there was, and always had been, a darker side to the Church's power. She did believe in something she could call God, but hers was an ever-present force in the universe, not the 'old man on a cloud' stereotype that had stayed with her since Sunday school, and made her question her own beliefs.

She did not get a chance to talk to Sylvie after the service but caught up with her at the reception in a nearby hotel.

"We didn't get much time to talk last night, Sylvie, but I don't suppose we will have more chance now – so many people want to see you. How are you coping with all the arrangements?   It all looks as if everything is effortlessly wonderful, but I expect you've had some awkward moments."

"Too right," Sylvie laughed, "just this morning there was a major panic about the flowers, but we managed to get it sorted out."

"Well, it all looks beautiful now," Maggie reassured `her.

The wedding venue was set with one long top table, for the bride, groom, bridesmaids, best man, and both sets of parents, but the remainder of the guests were seated at small round tables, which made the meal feel informal and more comfortable somehow. The top table had three huge vases of pink and white flowers spaced along its length, and each of the small ones had its own silvered glass container with flowers in a matching colour palette.

"When are you going back?" Sylvie asked.

"We thought we would have an extra day to pop up to London, and then go home the day after tomorrow."

"Come over for supper tomorrow night – we can have a real catch up then. You have never even met Tom properly, let alone had a chance to talk to Caroline – but she will be off on honeymoon then. Hopefully, our responsibility for all this will be over by then."

"We'd love to Sylvie if you are sure you won't be too exhausted. "And then hopefully the next time we meet you will be coming up to stay with us again. Sam would love to see you – he still remembers the trips up to London when he was small, and I think he still has the red London bus we bought him tucked away some-where!"

Chapter Twenty-Two

December 2019

The little girls, dressed as angels in white and silver, brought tears to Maggie's eyes. It was the same every year at the school Christmas nativity, whether she knew the young children or not. Just the sight of the little ones always made her well up. Even though she loved Sam dearly she had always longed for a little girl. Now she had one, in her grand-daughter, Emily, who had been so proud to take part in the school Nativity Concert.

Catrin was sitting in the audience with Maggie but encouraged the little ones on from her seat. She had finished work completely now, as the baby was due in a few weeks' time, but the children still looked to her for reassurance.

At the side of the stage, Opal sat at the piano, playing the carols, some in Welsh and some in English, to reflect the mix of parents in the audience. Someone (Catrin or Opal perhaps?) had even written some new songs for the children to sing, and they had obviously been very well rehearsed.

Maggie remembered the Christmas concerts when Sam was young. He was usually a shepherd, which meant his costume could be contrived quite easily out of pyjamas and tea-towels.

She was full of admiration for the mothers of the little girls, whose costumes were often stunning. This year, Emily's costume had been fashioned out of Ellie's wedding dress. The dress had been still hanging in the wardrobe in her old room, untouched for all the years in between. Now though, all the signs were that it was time to move on. Time, not to forget, but to stop putting everyone's life on hold because of what had happened in the past.

Maggie loved watching the little ones struggling valiantly through their various roles. After the nativity story, the older children joined in with singing the carols and the finale of the concert was a rousing chorus of 'O come all ye faithful', in which the audience were invited to join.

After the children left the stage, Mrs Lewis, the Head Teacher, thanked everyone for all their hard work, and asked the audience back for coffee and cake while the children changed back into their everyday clothes.

Catrin was busy chatting with her colleagues when the coffee was served, so Maggie took the opportunity to catch up with Opal when she came back into the hall.

"I really enjoyed that, Opal. Did you write some of the music?"

"Yes, a couple of the songs were mine. It is so lovely to be involved with the little ones and encourage them with music. I'm still helping out two or three days a week on a temporary basis but there may be a permanent vacancy for me soon."

"Have you decided what to do with your inheritance yet?"

Opal shook her head, "Still making up my mind. I want my mother to move up here, so I have put both her house and mine on the market and we will buy somewhere here for the two of us. Maybe if everything goes well and she gets a bit stronger, we can think about that holiday to Jamaica next year sometime. How are things with you? Are you still seeing Mike?"

"Yes, I think this is the real thing this time, Opal. He wants me to move in with him, but I am hesitating a bit. I am not sure about moving out of the Mill and giving up my independence. It was so hard trying to escape from my marriage to Paul, I am worried about committing again too completely. You are looking wonderful by the way."

Maggie could see that Opal's honey-coloured skin was glowing, whether from the joy of the performance, or something else. She had touched up the grey in her bouncy curls and looked at least ten years younger than when Maggie had seen her in the hospital.

"By the way," Opal added. "Paul came to see me a few weeks ago. As you know, at one time I would have been terrified of seeing him alone, but he seems to have changed so much since his accident at the waterfall."

Maggie looked doubtful as Opal continued.

"I saw him in the village shop one day and he seemed so contrite and anxious about me, that I agreed he could come over to the house. We had a really long chat, and he was so apologetic about his behaviour, I could not help but forgive him."

"Yes, he seems to have changed. He wants to play a big part in Sam and Catrin's life now and be a grandad to Emily and the new baby when it arrives, but I am still not sure I trust him completely even now."

Catrin came up to the two of them, coffee cup in hand.

"Do either of you two ladies fancy a top up?"

They both shook their heads.

"I'm full up on bara brith and Welsh cakes," Maggie protested. "Haven't got room for anything else. Actually, though, Catrin, I have thought of something. If time is on your hands during maternity leave, could you help me to find out more about my mum's side of the family? I know your Aunt Delyth has done a lot of work on your own family, and I would love to know more about our connection to this part of the world. From the minute I arrived here I felt at home, and I would love to know how we are connected with this place."

"What a great idea, Maggie! I would love to help, and I am sure Delyth would to. She has got about as far as she can with our own family tree, I believe. She did say, though, that is quite easy to get distracted and follow the wrong people back through generations before you realise you have made a mistake. Once she thought she had found an ancestor, but it turned out he emigrated to America, so he could not have been the one to carry the family line on here."

"I suppose it does get confusing the further you go back. But I would be grateful if we could perhaps plan it as a project together, at least before you get too busy with the new baby!"

After the concert, Maggie dropped Opal back at the cottage.

"Will you come in for a pre-Christmas drink, Maggie?"

"Well, I'm still stuffed with coffee and cake but perhaps I could manage a small glass of something. I haven't got far to drive home after."

"I've got some nice mini-liqueur bottles if you'd like one?"

"Do you know, Opal, that sounds a really nice idea. Might keep us in the Christmas spirit after the concert."

Maggie got out of the car and followed Opal into the house. She had not been inside since the Spring when they had called for some of Opal's things after her stay in hospital, and she was interested to see what Opal had done with the place.

Opal poured her a miniature of Tia Maria as they sat in the upstairs lounge with the curtains drawn back. It was pitch dark outside now but as they sat there the moon slowly began to climb up over the mountain top, softening the landscape with its pale, unearthly light. Maggie could see that Opal had added many homely touches to the cottage. The walls were hung with bright prints and tapestries and the log burner had kept the house cosy whilst they had been away at the concert.

"You've really made it nice here, Opal. I think you have put a lot of yourself into the place."

"To tell you the truth Maggie, I'm hoping I might persuade the landlord to sell it to me. It feels so much like home now, and as I told you before we have put my house and Mum's on the market now. If we can sell quite quickly, I am hopeful I might be able to persuade him to take advantage of a good cash offer. Once I buy somewhere, I will no longer be a tenant, and he might feel happier to sell the place than have to depend on the uncertain holiday-let income. He was certainly quick to let me take on a longer lease here, so I don't think his holiday-let bookings were bringing in the revenue he had hoped."

"So much depends on the weather here, Opal. We have found with the Mill that most of our lettings are in the Spring and Autumn. People still seem to want their summer fortnight in the sun, and Wales can't always provide that."

"There is something else I wanted to run through with you Maggie. I mentioned that Paul had been in touch and had apologised for his behaviour."

"You did indeed," Maggie suddenly thought she could guess what was coming.

"Well, he has changed so much now Maggie. His accident has made such a difference to him – he is a much less confident man now. Very unsure of himself, really. His own fall, coming so quickly after what happened to me, has really made him look at things completely differently. Anyway, we have become good friends over the last few weeks, and I think there is a possibility of our becoming more than friends. I just wanted to make sure that you would be okay with that?"

"Well, Opal, its completely up to you. I am not sure I could ever trust him again, myself, but he might have learnt a lot from what has gone on these last few months. As far as I am concerned, I would not think any less of you if you did decide to see more of Paul. In fact, I would wish you the best of luck. If he really has changed, then maybe he deserves a second chance at finding happiness. I certainly would not begrudge him that."

Maggie was silent for a while, taking in what Opal had told her. She was not sure exactly how she did feel, but she had now found happiness with Mike, who was she to stand in the way of Opal and Paul perhaps finding happiness too?

"Look at the time, I'd better be getting back," she said suddenly, coming out of her reverie.

She gave Opal a quick kiss on the cheek just to make sure Opal realised she meant what she had said, and then headed for the door.

* * * * *

February 2020

Thank goodness the floods had abated now, Maggie thought as she drove to the hospital in Wrexham. For several weeks there had been disruption to the valley routes due to the heavy rain. On some days during the month, all the main roads out of the valley had been blocked and only those who knew the back roads well could find a way through to Oswestry or Welshpool. At least her journey today did not involve any detours. The sky was still heavy, though, with low lying cloud hanging in misty white patches over the hills and promised further rain to come.

At least this time it was a happy journey, she thought. Catrin had given birth the day before to a brother to Emily and it was Maggie's first chance to see him.

Parking was difficult, as usual, in the hospital car park. Sometimes she felt that the Welsh policy of free parking at hospitals was open to abuse by people using the car park for other purposes. Finally, she found a space at the far end, nearer the shops than the hospital. It was quite a walk back up to the Maternity Ward, and she felt quite breathless by the time she arrived.

She pressed the entry bell by the ward door and waited to be admitted. After a few moments, a nurse arrived and pointed her towards Catrin's bed. The cubicles seemed awfully close together, with little privacy, but at least each one was curtained off from the rest of the ward. Sam and Catrin had wanted the baby to be registered as born in Wales, so had chosen Wrexham instead of Shrewsbury or Telford for the delivery.

Sam was there, beaming at her as she walked in. Delyth and Huw were looking after Emily for a few days, so Sam had stayed with Catrin overnight.

"Here he is," Sam showed off the baby proudly. "We are still deciding what to call him. We did not want to think of names too early, we were a bit superstitious I suppose. Catrin wants it to be a Welsh name as Emily's name is English."

"How about Owain," suggested Maggie "after the Welsh prince Owain Glyndwr. That is probably about as Welsh as you can get."

"It's a thought," Sam agreed.

Catrin nodded, "Yes Owain would be fine, but what about a second name – Huw, perhaps after my dad?"

"Owain Huw Johnson," mused Sam, "that sounds good."

"I rang Steve last night to give him the news. He was delighted and told me he was hoping he might be able to come over in the summer."

"Do you really think he might – he has never been near the place since …"

"Yes, well, I think things are a little different now. I had told him last summer about Amy Rae's visit. He feels happier about coming back now that we have all understood a lot more about Ellie's state of mind.

Perhaps he needs to come back here and face up to everything that happened so that he can finally put it behind him."

Catrin looked confused.

"Didn't Opal say that he had gone to America because he could not cope with the thought that Tristan had come back to him, was following him around?"

"Well, Amy has hopefully sorted that out now, hasn't she? Emily no longer talks about Trissi at all, does she?"

"No, I'm hoping her real friends at school have made her forget all about him. She seems happy enough these days, anyway, and has not said anything to make us worry about her lately. Here, would you like to hold the little one?"

Catrin handed the new baby to Maggie. She looked into his calm blue eyes and still face.

"He is so quiet, and seems very content," she murmured.

"He has just been fed," Catrin laughed, "but it was a Caesarean birth, and the midwife said babies are often calmer after that, it's less traumatic for them than having to fight their way out."

Maggie nodded, and then added:

"By the way, I have some other news for you. You know I have been seeing Mike Lane over the last few months? Well we have been getting on so well he has asked me to move in with him, and I have agreed, so you will have a lot more room to expand at the Mill. Room for several more children again!" she laughed.

Sam looked anxious.

"Are you sure about this Mum – you haven't really known him that long."

"Yes, I think so Sam. I do not want us to get married, at least not yet until we see how things go. It was too difficult for me trying to escape being married the first time."

"What has Dad said about it?" Sam still referred to Paul as Dad. He could not lose this part of his childhood.

"Oh, I think he wishes me well. He had hoped last autumn that we might get back together now that he appears to have changed so much since Opal's fall and his own accident, but I told him there was no chance of that. At least we are on amicable terms now, but I could never put myself under his control again, however changed he seems to be."

Maggie did not mention her conversation with Opal just before Christmas. Time enough for that to come to light later if Opal and Paul's relationship did become serious.

"Well good luck Mum, but don't be in too much of a hurry to move out. There will always be room for you at the Mill if you want to come back."

"That is good to know, Sam. And I will still come and help out with the paperwork a couple of days a week."

Just at that moment she was interrupted by the baby gurgling at her. He was too young to smile but it looked like it. She suddenly felt a rush of recognition. Was it that the baby reminded her of Sam when he was newborn, or was it something else? The feeling was so strong – could it be, was it possible - but she would not mention anything to the others, "Tristan?" she wondered.

CHAPTER TWENTY-THREE

APRIL 2020 SHREWSBURY

"Anything interesting in the post?" Rob was carrying two cups of coffee back into the bedroom as Amy climbed the stairs up from the office.

"A letter from Catrin, at the Mill. You remember I told you about going to see them last Spring?"

"Yes, I remember, but why a letter, why not an email like everyone else these days?"

Amy climbed back into bed and grabbed her coffee from the bedside table, still clutching the letter in her hand. Due to the Coronavirus lockdown there was no need to hurry to get up these days, and they might as well spend a comfortable few hours there as rush up to do anything.

Amy was still getting the occasional commission when she could help people remotely, either over the telephone or on-line but her work hardly counted as essential, at least not to the powers that be.

The Covid-19 lock-down had brought her relationship with Rob to a head, though. They had had to decide whether Rob moved in with her completely or they did not see each other at all for weeks. It had forced a decision she had been reluctant to commit to - partly due to Matthew, she realised.

Rob was her neighbour from the cottage three doors down. An aspiring actor, with a few small credits on stage and screen to his name, he kept the wolf from the door by working as a handyman/painter and he had done some small jobs for Amy when she first took over the lease on her property. He was still getting some requests for help with essential repairs, but there was no acting work whatsoever as all the theatres were now closed. The television work had dried up as well, while programme makers tried to work out how to make dramas while taking account of social distancing.

Amy and Rob's relationship had gone forward in gradual steps. They had become friends after his initial work on the cottage, and then, quite slowly, evolved into going for the occasional drink and eventually a real relationship. Amy had been holding back to begin with. She did not want to lose contact with Matthew, who had been her main support for so long. Eventually Matthew himself decided she must move on. One night as she was brushing her hair in front of the dressing table mirror, he appeared to her.

"Amy, I am going to stop coming to see you," he told her firmly.

"Matthew!! How can you? How can you leave me after so long?"

"It is time Amy. You remember when your mother and father told you they had to fade more into the background?"

"Yes, but that was different. I had met you at college then, and they wanted me to get on with my life and not dwell in the past all the time."

"Well this is exactly the same, Amy. You will never commit to a relationship with a living person while you are still in touch with me. I can never give you the life you really need and deserve. I will still be there for you occasionally, when things get bad, but I will not come at your bidding whenever you think you want to see me."

Amy had reluctantly agreed that he was right, although the thought of a new relationship scared her. It was the crisis with the virus that had decided the matter. She felt she could not go without seeing Rob for weeks at a time, and so the issue was settled, and he had moved into her small flat above the office. It was not ideal, as there was little room for two people, but at least it was a test of their new, fuller relationship. They had agreed that once the lock-down was over they could find somewhere larger to live. Rob had kept on his cottage just down the road, but as Amy needed her office still, they had decided that her home would be their base while the restrictions continued.

"So, what has Catrin got to say?" Rob asked.

"I'll read you the letter:

Dear Amy,

How are you managing in this difficult time? I hope it is not causing you too much hardship. I am not sure if Maggie has been in touch with you at all, but I had a baby in February, a brother for Emily. We are calling him Owain Huw.

I am on maternity leave now so the lock-down has not affected my working life, but we are all getting very bored. Obviously, the Mill complex is not having any holiday bookings now, but we are trying to keep busy with getting everything up to scratch for when the season can start again.

Maggie has moved out of the Mill now and is living with Mike Lane. He was the counsellor her sister Ellie was seeing just before she died. Maggie had been talking to him to find out more about her sister's feelings at the time and they became close – close enough to make a new start together. I wish them all the best, although Sam has reservations about it. I suppose sons always do worry if their mothers have new relationships.

I thought about what you had told me about Maggie's father but decided not to say anything at the time, while emotions were still so stirred up by what was happening at the Mill. I think now, though, that she is in a much happier place so it might be the time to tell her. Would you like to write to her and let her know what you told me last summer? She has Mike for support now so it might be a good time. I did tell her last year that you were having trouble contacting her father so that would explain the delay in letting her know.

Anyway, apart from bringing you up to date with the news ..."

"Ah, now we are getting to the real reason for the letter," Rob interrupted, pretending to grab it from Amy's hand. Amy pushed him away and continued reading.

"...something strange is happening. I expect you will understand straight away, but I wanted to discuss it with you.

Emily loves her little brother very much. She is very gentle and caring with him, but she just will not call him Owain. She keeps calling him "Trissi". I think I know what you will make of this, but Sam and I are very – 'grounded' shall we say? Anything that seems to suggest the paranormal is quite foreign to us.

Perhaps when this lock-down is over, you might come and see us all again. Just in case there are any issues that still need to be resolved.

There is one more thing, it's very strange but when I am alone in the evenings at the Mill, when the children are asleep and Sam is working late down in the office, there have been several occasions when I could swear I heard a train whistle, but the last train here ran in the 1960's and all the tracks have been torn up.

Sending you all our best wishes, love, Catrin"

"So, what do you make of it then, Amy Rae, Psychic Consultant?" Rob teased her.

"Well, to me, it is obvious Rob – although I know you are sceptical. When Tristan was given permission to move on, he had to go somewhere after all, didn't he?"

"What was that about the train whistle then?"

"Something to think about when I go to visit them again. Catrin is a strange girl. She seems so unapproachable about anything that verges on the paranormal in any way, but I think she is an empath, although she does not understand, or give way to her subconscious. I would very much like to get to know her better – we are about the same age after all."

"You just want an excuse to escape back to the Welsh hills," Rob teased, messing up her hair as he spoke.

"Well, it would be nice. Do you know that there are more sheep in Wales than people? Maybe when all this uncertainty is over, we can go together and I can tell you all about the area, and I would like to see Anna Humphreys at the B&B again. Ghosts and spirits apart, it is a very soothing place to visit. Perhaps when Shrewsbury has lost its appeal, we might even think about moving out there ourselves."

"Not just yet, though, love. It's too far away from my potential theatre work." Rob protested.

"Yes, but you never know what the future might hold, Rob. You might decide on a different career entirely." She pulled him back onto the bed, kissing him hard to stifle any more protests.

* * * * *

MAY 2020

Maggie had been pottering in the garden most of the day.

The early May weather had been wonderful the last few days and she and Mike had made the most of lockdown by redesigning the generous back garden that came with the cottage. Due to their efforts, it now included a vegetable plot with raised beds, made from a recycled garden table that had seen better days. Maggie had even grown some pepper seedlings from a yellow pepper she had used in cooking and could not wait to see if she could raise more peppers for free.

Everywhere had been so much quieter since lockdown. The birdsong sounded louder than it had ever done before, and the birds themselves seemed tamer. She had a family of blue tits tearing through the fat balls in her feeders and a very tame blackbird, as well as occasional visits from various finches.

This afternoon, she had been surprised to see a wren sitting on the power cables, shrilling loudly with a call that sounded very much like electrical interference. It had been answered by two similar calls in opposite directions, but those birds were hidden from her in the branches of the trees in the adjoining fields.

She loved being in the garden. When she lived at the Mill she had pottered about with summer bedding and prettying up the place but it was only really since lockdown that she felt she had made a real connection with the garden, and the teeming wildlife around her. Just the feel of the soil in her fingers helped her to feel literally more grounded and at peace than she had every felt before. Of course, she realised, Mike had a lot to do with that feeling. She did feel however that she was now connecting in a much stronger way with the whole of nature. As she had mentioned to Mike only the evening before, people and plants had a great deal in common.

"We all need water, and we all need sun-light, otherwise nothing would exist at all."

Mike had nodded in agreement and then added thoughtfully,

"Have you noticed the way the plants always grow towards the light? Perhaps we should take a lesson from that."

"We should reach for the light too, you mean?"

"Something like that," Mike looked embarrassed, "but it can't do any harm to look on the bright side, can it?"

At four o'clock Mike had popped down to the village shop and post office for some extra milk and came back with a letter for Maggie.

"They were holding this for you at the Post Office," he told her, "They weren't sure whether to send it down to the Mill or let us have it here so the postman left it there for the time being. He knew one or other of us would be in before too long."

Maggie looked at the envelope curiously. She did not recognise the writing, which was large, flowing, and confident.

She opened it hesitantly, not sure what might lay inside.

"It's from Amy Rae," she told him as she started to read.

"Why is she writing to us now?"

"When she was here last Spring, I asked her if she could contact my dad. He died in an accident at a tube station when I was seventeen. I don't think I ever told you before – we were always too busy talking about Ellie, somehow – although I believe in a way it was all connected in Ellie's mind when she did what she did........ Apparently, he had been rushing for a train and was anxious to make a connection at Liverpool Street. When he got onto the platform and a tube train was about to depart, he had tried to push the doors open with the tip of his umbrella. The umbrella had become stuck in the door, but the doors had not opened, and Dad was dragged into the tunnel. No-one could really understand why that train was so important. There would have been another one in a few minutes, after all. The guard had seen what had happened, and the train stopped almost straightaway, and reversed out of the tunnel, but he had been too severely injured, and was dead on arrival at hospital."

"How awful!", Mike interrupted.

"Yes, it was – it was terrible at the time. I never wanted to travel on a tube train ever again after that, but I had to sometimes. Anyway, I had asked Amy to find out if she could why he had been at that station which was miles from his normal route home. Last summer, Catrin told me Amy could not reach him, but apparently now she has."

"Whatever does she say?"

"Well it was always a bit of a mystery why he was in that place at that time, but when Sylvie came to Ellie's funeral, she did give me a hint of it, I suppose."

"In what way ?"

"She said there had been a strange woman at Dad's funeral who acted oddly. She and her mother had often talked about it, although they did not say anything at the time. From what Amy says here in her letter, Dad had been having an affair and was planning to leave us and set up home with this other woman. He had just come from her flat when he had the accident at the tube station."

"Oh Maggie! Is it a terrible shock?"

"Well, no, I suppose not really. What Sylvie told me after Ellie's funeral had always been at the back of my mind somewhere, I suppose. It is not the shock it could have been. Thank goodness Ellie knew nothing about it though. She always hero-worshipped Dad. She would have been devastated. It just seems so strange that all these old mysteries are coming to a head at the same time."

"Life has a way of working out, eventually, I suppose."

"Maybe, but although this isn't the shock it could have been, I still feel rather wobbly."

"Come and sit down and I'll make a cup of tea, my love."

Maggie's face had suddenly grown pale and Mike was quite worried about her. Even if, deep down, she had realised there was something odd about her father's death, it was still a shock for her to actually find out that he had been having an affair, and even perhaps planning to leave her mother, herself and Ellie. Always supposing that what Amy Rae had told her was true. Mike was never completely sure what he felt about psychic consultants, although Amy did seem to have brought matters to a head at the Mill, and hopefully allowed Maggie to move on with her life.

As he brought the tea into the cosy living room that overlooked the lane outside, he told her what he had been thinking.

"I've been going over and over in my mind what happened with Ellie, all those years ago, and I realised something. I do not think she was ever diagnosed, but I believe she was bi-polar, or what used to be called 'manic-depressive'. Bi-polar people can be extremely high and excitable one minute and then incredibly low and depressed the next – they often have dramatic mood swings. I know all of us feel some responsibility for what happened – you, me, Opal, Steve, Paul – but many of us go through times in our lives when things seem very bleak and desperate. Most of us can find the resilience within ourselves to believe that if times are bad now, they may well get better soon. Ellie obviously could not find that hope in her heart at that particular time, and just acted by instinct, ruled by her illness."

"That would make sense, Mike. She had dramatic mood swings. Sometimes she would be so excited it was difficult to cope with, and then at others it was as if she was hiding away in a different place from the rest of us and we could not get through to her."

"That is what I mean, I suppose. I do not know that there was anything any of us could have done to prevent what happened. Once it was in her mind, that was it, really."

They were quiet for a moment, their minds once more filled with Ellie, and then Mike made a decision.

"As soon as all this lockdown is over, we must have a few days away somewhere. Where do you fancy going? I don't suppose we will be able to go anywhere too far away for a while until this virus is more under control."

"I've always fancied another trip to the Wye Valley," she considered, "I went there with Mum and Dad in my teens – I think we had a camping trip down there. I expect its quite different now."

"Maybe, but there is plenty of lovely countryside to explore down there – and its near to Tintern Abbey. I have always wanted to see that. I did some historical research about it while I was at college, but never found the time to visit the place. We could hire a camper van and explore that whole area if you wish?"

"What a great idea, Mike. I'll look forward to it."

`* * * * *

Later that evening, Mike called out to her from the back door of the cottage.

"It's a beautiful night – come and have a look."

She came out from the kitchen, tea towel in hand, and joined him in gazing at the stars. The clear sky was amazing. The night was a little chilly, with a hint of frost, but the full moon on one side of the sky, and bright Venus almost exactly opposite, seemed to be competing as to which one was the most beautiful. Towards the west, the shining silver-gilt disc of Venus hung almost like a lantern in the deepening night.

"Such a shame we could not have got the Dark Skies project completed before the lockdown," Maggie murmured,

"People from the city would just adore our night skies here."

"Just as well, though," Mike was practical. "If it had been finished, and bookings taken, you would have had to cancel them all anyway."

"Yes, you're right. And if we had borrowed money to renovate the old stables and install that telescope we have always been planning, we would not have been able to meet the payments on the loan without income from the visitors. I do miss my two days a week over at the Mill though. I hope we can all get together again soon. It is so hard not to be able to see the children, especially. I know we have been doing video calls, but it is not the same as being able to give Emily a hug and see how little Owain is getting on – he must be getting quite big by now. I can't wait to hold him again." Maggie gave a sudden shiver as the cold air began to get uncomfortable.

"This will all pass Maggie. Things will eventually get back to normal, and at least it has made us all appreciate the good things we have, and how lucky we are."

Maggie gave him a hug.

"I don't know how I would have got through this without you Mike."

"You mean you don't regret moving out from the Mill? If you had still been living there, you could still have seen them all."

"No, Mike, I don't regret anything at all. I am perfectly happy being in lockdown with you. But I do worry about the future and what will happen to us all."

"Don't worry, Maggie, things will work out, one way or another. After all, to quote that hackneyed old saying 'life is a journey, not a destination', and maybe we all need shaking up a bit, so that we do not take everything for granted. Sometimes the cosmos has ways of shocking us into other ways of seeing things, making us realise just what are the important things in life."

Maggie stood at his side, squeezing his hand. She moved in close in the chilly air, and they watched as Venus gradually moved down towards the summit of the hill, and then sank out of sight.

As they turned to go back into the house, Mike suddenly stopped.

"What's the matter, my love?" Maggie was anxious.

"Oh, it's okay – it's just that I could have sworn just then that I heard, clearly from across the valley, the sound of a train whistle."

"But there haven't been any trains for at least 60 years!"

"Yes, I know, my love. Strange isn't it?"

- Ends –

Author's note

Nant-y-felin is a fictional range of buildings set somewhere in the Tanat Valley in North Powys. All the characters in the book are also completely fictional, with the exception of the two dogs, Mindy and Bonny, who have both been my companions over the years.

I believe that all of us at sometime in our lives experience something we cannot completely explain. I have been aware of two ghosts myself, one a young woman in the house where I now live, and the other a dog at the local Inn. Neither of them was frightening or threatening in any way.

The voice in Maggie's head in her dream, "Swim, you idiot", was also something I experienced as a 10-year-old in a real, near drowning experience. Also, when my second child was born and I saw him for the first time, I felt I recognised his 'soul' or whatever you would like to call it. I have no idea who it was I recognised, only that I had known that person before.

I hope you enjoyed the book and found it reassuring, rather than unsettling. It was not my intention to frighten anyone!

Lightning Source UK Ltd.
Milton Keynes UK
UKHW012230221120
373896UK00001B/37